ROOM

FOR

ANOTHER
HEART

Yvonne C. Hebert, MA

iUniverse, Inc.
Bloomington

ROOM FOR ANOTHER HEART

iUniverse books may be ordered through booksellers or by contacting:

iUniverse
1663 Liberty Drive
Bloomington, IN 47403
www.iuniverse.com
1-800-Authors (1-800-288-4677)

Because of the dynamic nature of the Internet, any web addresses or links contained in this book may have changed since publication and may no longer be valid. The views expressed in this work are solely those of the author and do not necessarily reflect the views of the publisher, and the publisher hereby disclaims any responsibility for them.

Any people depicted in stock imagery provided by Thinkstock are models, and such images are being used for illustrative purposes only.

Certain stock imagery © Thinkstock.

ISBN: 978-1-4759-4275-0 (sc)
ISBN: 978-1-4759-4276-7 (ebk)

Library of Congress Control Number: 2012914038

Printed in the United States of America

iUniverse rev. date: 08/22/2012

Contents

Dedication

This book is dedicated to every person
who has stopped the abuse of humans or animals
through intervention or education.

Preface

Dear Reader:

Thank you for considering my book as your companion for a few hours. I want to chat with you a little before you start reading this story.

Moving to Los Angeles was one of the most exciting things I have ever done. For years, I was thrilled by the ocean, by the eternally blue sky, by the enormous energy of the city, and by the never ending places to go and things to do. But the day came when I recognized that I had become homesick for the seasons, the rivers, lakes, and woods of my childhood. I returned to Michigan for a visit that stretched into years.

I found a home in the Manistee National Forest and settled into it with my two collies and a cat. Many of my neighbors and their families had lived in their homes for eighty, even a hundred years, and more.

Even though I was surrounded by trees and streams for several miles outside of the nearest town, I thought it wouldn't be that different from living in the suburbs of a city. But I was really wrong. Yes, there was electrical and telephone service. For several years internet was dial up only, and there were just four channels available on television. No Satellite. No Cable. Water came from a well through a pipe 140 feet into the ground, and propane for heat had to be trucked to my home.

The biggest surprise was the forest animals. Somewhere in my mind, I knew that a forest would have wild critters, but I didn't expect to find bobcats roosting on my car at night, and bears sleeping on my porch and looking in my door. I expected rabbits and raccoons, even possums, but bald eagles, wild turkeys and coyotes?

One evening, I looked out my window and there among my flowers was a gorgeous, long-haired, white cat with the fluffiest tail I had ever seen on a feline. I saw, after a minute of watching, that it had a rather large, black spot on its side. I couldn't remember ever seeing it in the neighborhood before and was pondering where it had come from when it turned, lifted its head from beneath some flowers, and stared into my eyes. Its little, black, skunk face, tiny eyes boring into mine, looked startled but hardly as startled as mine.

I had always thought skunks were black with a white stripe or two, but there it was. I learned later that it was a spotted skunk. I had never heard of, or conceived of, a spotted skunk. I was to learn that most of what I had learned about wild animals failed to describe them in anything but the sketchiest of terms.

That animals are creative, independent and awe-inspiring is hardly a common belief, but my experiences with these creatures have been some of the most important in my life. When my collies passed on, I adopted two shelter dogs that you will meet in this book. I wondered how to tell the story of some of these animals in an interesting way. The answer came as the Afghanistan and Iraq wars affected my life, mostly through the lives of my clients.

As a psychologist, I have worked with people who were traversing the pitfalls of loneliness, grief, and disability; of abandonment, abuse, and betrayal; of courage, decision and love in its many, many forms.

I became privy to the story of a young soldier who had no one to care for his pet dog when he left for his tour of duty. His beloved pet of several years became an unhappy resident of an animal shelter in a nearby town. He left for his military commitment grieving the abandonment of his best friend, only too aware of his pet's probable fate.

At the same time, I saw an economic recession hitting the state and the nation. A story formed in my mind. I hope you like it. The animal stories are all true. The rest of the story is fiction.

I'm hoping that in reading my book, people will understand that there are many ways to support our military with the hardships involved in their service to our country. Caring lovingly and responsibly for the pets of deployed military people when they have no one to care for them is one way that we can show our concern.

Again, thanks for picking up my book. I hope it speaks to you. I hope you love reading it.

Yvonne C. Hebert
5/19/12

1

The Dream

Late spring. The cold was gone from the land but not from my heart. Spring rains had turned the snow to slush and the ground into sludge. The warming sun had dried the mud. Buds had burst into green leaves and colorful blossoms, but my spirit still felt frozen. My heart encased in ice. My insides felt like a hard, hurting rock.

Sitting in my sunroom, as I had on so many mornings since the Army sedan had pulled into my driveway, I watched, expressionless, as a mother deer quietly ate the buds from the rose bushes along the side of my house. In the early morning light, her dark, tawny shape appeared as a sculpture against the green world around her.

I tried not to feed on the jealousy that twisted in my heart as I watched her speckled twin fawns cavorting about the lawn, mindful only of the joy of movement. The fawns bucked and twisted playfully. Their spindly legs and knobby knees were flying, their tiny black hoofs flashing.

Closer to me, the movement of a wasp caught my eye. It was a really big wasp, and a very patient wasp, working its way along the eaves at the side of my house. It appeared to be looking for an opening into the roof.

"That wasp's diligence should put me to shame," I thought. "It's about its life, whatever that is."

The seconds stretched into minutes, and the minutes ticked by unchecked by either of us. The wasp pored over every inch of the wood. Every crack was examined and re-examined before it moved on to scour another area.

A few inches below it, on the underside of the eave it was currently navigating, was a small hole, a good inch square. I had seen it last summer and meant to fix it, but like so many things these days, it had remained neglected.

Watching, I wondered idly if that hole would become home for a wasp nest just a few feet from a door that was used constantly.

"Rats!" I thought. "I'll be chasing wasps in the house." But no, the wasp had had enough. It circled the eaves it had been inspecting. Once. Twice. Enough. It disappeared into the rose bushes below.

I wanted to stop looking at the eaves, but I couldn't. I stared at them, wondering if there was a way into a more promising future for me that I was missing. I, too, was tired of looking. Tired of examining the world, of scratching at every apparent opportunity, of being pleasant to people I didn't know. I was tired of the smiling mouths and the curious eyes as their heads swung to and fro; tired of another "no, not today."

Their eyes were never matter of fact but always curious. Why? What were they watching for? My reaction to their rejection? What did they think I would do? Laugh? Cry? Throw something? Or somehow show that I recognized the power they were pretending to be subtle about owning?

It didn't matter. I couldn't make myself go out again, at least, not for a while. Maybe someday . . . maybe someday I would try again.

★ ★ ★

My dreams that night were frightening. The wasp was there, of course. Black and gold, with shiny wings, its head strangely detached from that long, slender body. There were openings, so many openings, holes in walls that turned out to be shadows. Huge oak doors, screen doors, white cottage doors, steel doors, always locked tight after appearing to be open at least a crack. It seemed as if some doors were standing wide open until I rushed up to them. Then I would find the door was locked and the apparent opening just a darkness that disappeared as I approached.

Windows were stuck tight, painted shut, nailed down. Window after window, I struggled with each of them, desperately trying to push one open. Finally I even tried to break a window's glass, anything to get through, to escape. The wasp circled near me, often times walking on the walls, scouring the surface of my dream. I felt threatened, frightened.

When my dream shifted gradually to the inside of a nicely-furnished, peaceful house, I breathed a sigh of relief. But as I went about the house getting acquainted with it, I realized there were no rooms. There were only walls—straight walls and slowly curving walls. No windows. No doors. The peaceful house was starting to darken ominously. The quietness now felt cold, lifeless, deceptive.

I woke in a cold sweat, my heart thumping wildly, anxiety pounding the inside of my head. I staggered out of bed and headed toward the kitchen and a glass of water. My mouth felt so dry it could have been sandpaper.

"My blood pressure must be two hundred over a hundred," I thought wryly, opening the fridge.

Water glass in hand, I headed for the living room and the noise of the TV. I didn't want to go to sleep again. I didn't want to dream again. I didn't want to think at all. I felt fear clutching at my throat, sending chills across my shoulders. An exquisite sense of weakness coursed through my bowels.

★ ★ ★

The darkness of the night was just starting to be diluted with the first rays of the morning sun when I woke Moose.

"Let's go for a walk," I said, jiggling his bed.

Moose stretched luxuriously without rising. One brown eye opened and stared at me, questioning, a little unbelieving.

"Well, I'm going for a walk," I turned and headed slowly for the door.

Moose stretched again, and I heard a low, moaning groan.

"Must be nice to feel that relaxed," I thought dryly.

But his black toenails could be heard clicking on the cold floor behind me as I walked through the kitchen to the back door.

I didn't bother with a leash. Moose would stay close to me. And he did. His lumbering, black body barely visible in the dim light, he nosed his way down the road with me a few feet behind.

It felt good to be outdoors in the cool air, especially after the nightmares of the previous night. For reasons I didn't understand, I felt more alive than I had in months.

At the two-track that led around my property, Moose didn't hesitate but veered off the road, his feet padding silently along the tire tracks. At first I found myself staring at the uneven ground, intent on not losing my balance in the early light of dawn. But Moose was hard to ignore, snuffling excitedly, busily exploring the thick, shadowy brush overgrown along the sides of the wide path.

I remembered the winter when I had driven with my fiancé, Chase Maslin, through these woods and the fields around our property to lay the two-track.

"To mark our digs," he had said, laughing.

I hung onto the jeep's frame as he roared around and around the area, snow flying, weeds and bushes crushing under the tires.

At times he would stop and say, "Does it stay or go?" and we would look critically at the tree or trees that had loomed up in front of us. Most of the time, we had figured a way to go around the bigger trees, but on occasion he would climb out of the jeep, pick up the chain saw and fell the smaller ones.

Usually I waited in the jeep, loving watching him, his broad back holding the saw with ease, his brown hair barely showing under his parka hood. Face red from the exertion, he would climb back into the jeep, cold and perspiring at the same time, his blue eyes bright with energy, rubbing his hands together for warmth. I would hand him a cup of hot chocolate from the thermos we carried in the jeep, and we would take a few "us" moments before setting off again.

We had such big plans for our lives together. We had found the perfect old farm house on thirty acres of land in the Manistee Forest. Our home had ten acres of cleared land, the big farm house, a pole barn, and an animal barn. The rest of the property was a thick pine forest adjacent to state forest land that teemed with wild life.

Bear Creek, named for the many black bears that were seen in the area, ran through the far corner of our land. A tributary of the swift-running Manistee River, the creek was alive with trout and drew deer and many other animals to drink.

"Close enough to go fishing but far enough away that we won't have mosquitoes in our back yard," Chase had observed optimistically.

We were going to build a small bridge over the water—very romantic. A place where the kids could play while Chase fished and I put out the picnic lunch and relaxed.

Chase was working on his BA in History and driving a truck for a warehouse in nearby Traverse City. He moved into the old farmhouse and started the renovations so that we could move in after our wedding, planned for the next summer. Our future had seemed secure since I was almost finished with my teaching degree.

But almost imperceptibly hard times hit our area. Jobs were drying up in the towns around our home, and Chase found himself called to work less and less. He hunted for jobs to stay even with his bills but found nothing he could count on. Even keeping our home was being threatened by the economic shift in our area.

Chase had surprised me one day with a picnic lunch. I looked at the fried chicken, potato salad, and coconut meringue pie tucked away in his mom's picnic basket and frowned skeptically.

"So what's the occasion, Mr. Maslin? You've gone all out here."

"It's the best of Syd's Deli," Chase laughed. "And it is a special occasion."

He wouldn't tell me more until we were comfortably settled in the grass on the edge of Bear Creek. For a few minutes, we sat eating fried chicken and listening to the birds and the gurgling of the waters rushing over the rocks in the creek.

"Cathy," Chase reached out for my hand. "We need to talk about our plans."

Chase's voice had become so serious that an uneasy feeling touched my soul. I hesitated a moment to collect my thoughts and then looked into his eyes, normally so filled with laughter, now so unusually sober.

"I'd like to get married right away, Cathy."

"OK," I said, with a little laugh that hinted of anxiety.

His statement should have filled me with joy, but the tone of his voice did nothing to calm the nervous feelings that were flooding me.

"I'm ready when you are," I stated without hesitation. "I do wonder what the rush is, though."

"You're not going to like this," he explained. "But I think I need to enlist in the Army. I can't make enough to earn a living the way things are right now. I've only had a couple calls to work this week. It doesn't look like there's going to be much more work for a while. Classes will be out in a couple of months." He stopped, searching for the right words.

"You're right, Chase," I said, trying to keep the hysteria out of my voice. "I don't like it."

"Honey, I need to do this," he leaned toward me, his voice husky, urgent. "I'm getting behind in my bills. We could lose the house. And we've both put everything we've saved into it."

I looked into his eyes, so blue, so earnest, and my heart jerked. My mouth felt dry, and the muscles of my shoulders had tightened like a vise.

"I love you, Chase," I said slowly. "I can lose the house. I can't lose you. I don't care if I never have a house of my own. I do care that wherever I am, you're there too."

"Cathy, Honey, I'll only be gone for a little while. A year, it's just a few months. I'm not going to leave you forever. I love you too, Cathy. I always will. But this gives me a way to earn a living until things loosen up here. It's a chance to learn skills that may help me find a job when I get back. I can find out what's really going on over there, too."

Listening to him, I could feel tears welling up in my eyes. My stomach had begun to feel nauseous, and an ugly taste was creeping into my mouth. I felt a sudden surge of anger at his inability to understand what I was saying.

"We're not just talking about a job, Chase. We're talking about your life," I snapped. "Your life matters to me. We'll handle the money somehow."

"Getting hurt's a possibility, Cathy, but not a big one. The majority of people come back just fine. It's like one in tens of thousands, maybe more, don't make it. Those are pretty good odds, you have to admit."

He was going. I could feel his determination. There was nothing more that I could say. I remained horrified at his plans, but after that conversation I tried to keep my objections unemotional. I didn't want to quell his excitement. He did, after all, have to live with his choice for many months ahead.

We were married two weeks later. Not the elaborate affair we had talked of earlier but still a beautiful, if simple, wedding. I wore my mother's wedding dress. Our minister cleared a time for us in the church, and we had the reception on the church grounds. Chase's brother, Derek, drove up from Ann Arbor to be his best man. My best friend, Bea Stimson, dropped everything to help me with the details and to be my matron of honor.

Our parents said later that it was a classic, sweet, old fashioned wedding. We assumed that meant they were pleased. It didn't matter to us. We were married.

The only problem we had was the specter of Chase joining the Army soon, which he did a couple of months later. Much to my chagrin, Chase came back from boot camp thrilled at his decision, even talking of making the Army a career.

"It's going to be ok," Chase reassured me, sensing my lack of enthusiasm. "The Army trained us really well. I'm prepared for anything. The war in Iraq won't last forever. I'll be home in a year."

I tried to smile, to be happy for him, but a year can be a very long time. Life changing events can happen in a second, even when the year is almost over. Chase didn't make it back to me.

I was frozen with grief for months. Chase had been away for so long it was hard to comprehend that he really was never coming home again. Officers came to the house to tell me that Chase was gone and what had happened, but at the time I couldn't fully comprehend what they were saying. They gave me a letter with the details for me to read later, but I never did.

I didn't want to understand the details of how that strong, beautiful body that I loved to watch and touch could be shattered, how the energy and life force I lived to share could disappear, the smiling eyes be closed forever. I haven't read that letter yet.

At Chase's funeral, I felt both frozen and hysterical. It was a military funeral. I took the flag, starring past the officer. My eyes riveted on the steel brown coffin, my mind numb. The gun salute echoed through my being in waves of shock, of finality. I felt the deepest, sharpest pain tear through my heart and chest. Hot tears slid mercilessly down my face. And then I heard the words, whispered to me by someone behind me.

"Cathy, be brave. Chase is a hero."

"Chase was a hero to me," I said quickly, my voice louder than I intended, "before he ever put on a uniform."

Tears burned again on my face as the memories flashed past. That wasn't the end of the hard times. The recession hit big time soon after and my own job as an English teacher got cut in the first wave of cut backs at the School District.

There were many apologies made, considering I had just lost Chase, but rules were rules. Last hired. First fired. There were promises made for rehiring, but the recession only got worse. The state cut even more funds from the school districts as families, seeking work, began moving to more prosperous states.

I shook the tears off my face and tried to keep Moose's meandering rear in sight. Chase had bought him for me as a wedding present.

"What kind of dog is he?" I asked timidly, trying to catch the wiggling, black puppy into my arms. "He looks like he's going to get awfully big."

"I hope he gets big!" Chase laughed. "You're going to be out here by yourself while I'm gone. He's Lab and Great Dane, maybe something else too. He's a puppy, eight weeks. You'll be the biggest thing in his life."

"Chase! Eight weeks! He has to weigh thirty pounds right now," I looked into the soulful, brown, puppy eyes, knowing I was hooked. "Look at the size of his feet!"

Chase was delighted with Moose. The few months the three of us had together were marked in my memory with love, laughter, puppy type accidents, and the kind of bumbling that only a huge puppy could manage.

Well, Moose reached a fighting weight of one hundred and thirty pounds. At that weight, he discovered he could pretty much go anywhere he wanted and eat anything he wanted—including possums, raccoons, and deer parts. I assumed, perhaps wrongly, that he had found these creatures dead alongside the road.

At one point he had been deathly ill from a bacterial, gastric infection.

"This has to be from something he ate," the vet advised me.

Knowing Moose, I assumed it was probably something from a nearby swamp that had been dead for a very long time. That illness hit my pocket book, but didn't change his eating habits.

Moose had gained a good fifteen pounds over the last summer and was less active than he had been, for which I was grateful. He was staying closer to home, which made him a better companion to me, at least when the wanderlust didn't strike him.

At such times, Moose seemed to feel obliged to bring at least part of his hunt home. I had found no less than two whole rabbits, and parts of a third, on my living room floor during the previous year. I did such hysterical screaming each time that he finally seemed to get the message that he didn't need to share with me.

After one particularly grueling and unsuccessful job hunting effort, I returned home drained and despondent. Moose didn't greet me at the front door as he usually did, and I wandered through the house to my bedroom. I found him curled up comfortably in the middle of my bed chewing on a deer leg. His eyes were clearly innocent of any forbidden behavior and very surprised to see me.

I had let out a blood-chilling scream and lunged at him, but he was already past me, the deer leg grasped tightly in his mouth. How he had gotten around me with that three-foot-long deer leg and out the doggy door without my once connecting with his black hide still has me wondering. I had whirled around to chase him, but the doggie door in the kitchen was already slapping shut behind him. Enraged, frustrated, I had sworn to kill Moose as soon as I could get my hands on him.

The delicate bedspread, pale pink and beige, crocheted rows holding the hand-stitched cloth patterns together, was a total mess. Crafted by my great aunt, now gone, it had always been one of my most precious treasures. I tore the muddy, bloody bedspread and a couple blankets off the bed and carried them to the car, fuming. It was a job for the cleaners, not me.

On the way back into the house, I saw Moose peering at me from behind an enormous pine tree, his brown eyes curious and scared, his otter-like tail waving slowly, hopefully. I thought of Chase's love for the dog, my heart melted, and Moose lived to misbehave another day.

★　★　★

The sky was fully ablaze with morning light when we reached Bear Creek. The previous spring I had placed an old, wooden chair by the side of a gnarled, weathered oak near the widest part of the stream. I brushed the twigs and leaves off the chair seat and sat down, watching the current rushing between and over the stones and rocks in the bed of the stream.

It wasn't deep here, but it was very cold, clear water. Oblivious to the frigid wetness, Moose tramped across the stream to the other side. Bent on new discoveries, his nose searched through the weeds and brush as if he were tracking the most elusive of prey.

I wondered idly what would have happened to Moose if Chase and I had not been a couple. Who would have been there to take care of him when Chase left for Iraq?

His parents, of course, would have cared for the dog. But they liked to travel and he would have inhibited that part of their lives. Would they have kept him when Chase was gone forever? They had never really liked big dogs, had never made an effort to get to know Moose. They had laughed at his antics as a puppy when his feet were too big for his legs and nothing about him had seemed coordinated.

"I always wanted my own dog," Chase had said, sitting on the floor, cuddling the sleeping puppy, and smiling up at me. I remembered now that Chase had said they had never had a dog when he was growing up. They'd never had a cat either. No, his parents wouldn't have kept Moose.

"His getting the dog was an act of growth away from his parents," I understood slowly, "perhaps even defiance." I wondered if other young people behaved that same way.

"Of course they did," I answered myself. It would have been a natural kind of rebellion, of asserting authority over what they could and couldn't do.

So what did soldiers do with their pets when they were called to service? What about people in the National Guard who had never expected to be in a fighting war or far from home for any length of time? What did they do with their pets if they didn't have a family who could care for the animal for a year or more?

My musing was cut short when Moose thundered back across the stream, spraying a shower of water in all directions. I leaped off the chair and dashed behind the trunk of the oak, trying to avoid the drenching I could see was coming.

Moose mistook my flight as a time to play and bounded joyfully after me, his face contorted in a goofy grin. He stopped only long enough to shake himself hard in front of me!

Oh, that water was so cold!

2

New Beginnings

I was up before dawn the next morning. After feeding Moose, I took my own breakfast into the sunroom. This cheerful, cozy room had become my favorite retreat, especially in the morning. I could watch the sun coming up, and the turkeys float down out of the trees where they had roosted for the night.

I had watched in awe the first time I had seen these huge birds flap their way into the upper reaches of some maples at the side of my yard. Their wings didn't seem to be large enough or strong enough to lift their bulky bodies into the air. To my astonished delight, they soared slowly upward with all the grace and power of a heavily loaded cargo plane.

Coming down from the trees they would appear to be strongly affected by gravity. In reality, they landed easily with their wings spread, apparently for drag, and ready for the day's work of searching the forest floor for food. They would spend most of the daylight hours on the ground in little family groups.

The turkeys would start with breakfast under the bird feeders, picking up seeds dropped by the little birds. If I went outside while they were in the yard, they would sidestep slowly into the forest without apparent fear, but watching me closely and with the utmost curiosity.

Moose lay devotedly a few feet away, alternately watching me and dozing, his black head between his pancake paws. As I looked at him, I wondered again about the fate of the pets of military people with no available resources for pet care. I knew Chase would have been devastated if he had had to take Moose to a shelter and leave him to face an unknown future.

"John Dunnom would know the answer," I told myself with a sense of certainty.

Today, I had a list of errands I needed to accomplish, but I was determined to make a stop in Traverse City to visit with John. A life-long friend of Chase's, John Dunnom ran the Army recruiting office. It was he who had convinced Chase his future was in the Army. In my book, he owed me big time.

★ ★ ★

Driving through Traverse City, the sun was high overhead as I passed Front Street, a lively street with extraordinarily heavy pedestrian traffic. I usually liked to study the many tourists walking there and guess what state they called home. I often wondered if the tourists were able to perceive the resilient spirit of Michigan people from the sturdy, winter-ready buildings they were seeing and the many unique, handcrafted wares being sold in the shops.

When the coast loomed in the distance, I felt a sense of anticipation wondering how the lake would appear. The water of the lake changed color constantly, depending on the sun's brightness, the temperature, the wind, or some other whim of nature.

Reaching the Coast Highway, Grand Traverse Bay lay as far as my eye could see. Today it was a brownish-blue near the shore, then a bright green shade of turquoise for a good three hundred feet. But beyond, the deepest marine blue spoke to the depth of the lake's bay. Almost out of vision, green fingers of land cuddled the bay on either side of its mouth out into Lake Michigan.

The Coast Highway is also home to the Army Recruiting Office, where I planned to confront John. I hadn't been able to shake the question from my mind about soldier's pets. Chase had fallen in love with Moose on sight. He had asked about him every time we talked and in every letter home.

I questioned how a soldier could go into a war zone knowing he had just left his beloved pet, perhaps of many years, at a shelter or in some other situation with an uncertain future. It seemed to me that such a soldier would be emotionally distressed at being forced to choose between his pet and his promise to serve.

Having that kind of conflict resting in one's mind didn't sound to me like a good way to be entering a life or death situation. Perhaps I was a little too obsessed about this concern, but I wanted an answer. It was hardly a secret, to me or anyone that knew me, that I was emotional and obsessed about almost everything these days.

★   ★   ★

John jumped to his feet from behind his shiny, naked desk when I appeared in the doorway.

"Cathy," he exclaimed. "What brings you up here? Ready to enlist?"

"Oh, sure," I retorted sourly. "I can see that happening."

He flinched openly and grimaced, but held out his hand in greeting.

"Well, it's nice to see you again."

I stared at him, my chin set.

"Why had he come back without a scratch and Chase…?" I didn't let myself finish the thought.

Taking a deep breath, I tried to smile, to be the Cathy he was used to talking to when I was with Chase

"I thought maybe we could talk a little."

"Right," moving quickly, apparently relieved to have the conversation shifting, he pulled a chair toward the desk, inviting me to sit down.

The chair was wooden and hard. No cushion. No frills in this office. A couple of recruiting posters and a huge, three-month calendar hung on the walls. The telephone and a closed computer notebook graced his otherwise empty desk. A file cabinet stood lonesomely in the corner of the room. A couple of chairs were lined against a wall. Nowhere did I see a speck of dust.

His uniform was pressed stiff. His tie looked like it was choking him. His hair was cut so close to his head that it was hard to tell whether it was black or dark brown.

He sat behind his desk, his hands clasped together, waiting, watching me looking at him, and finally cleared his throat a little.

"I'm really torn up about Chase," he offered quietly. "I miss him a lot. It must be tough for you."

"I'm doing OK," I lied. "I wanted to talk to you about Moose."

"He's a big one," John smiled. "Too much for you to handle? Need to find him a new home?"

"No. No. Nothing like that. I wouldn't give Chase's dog away."

I felt suddenly awkward, trying to find the right words.

"It's just . . . I was thinking . . . wondering . . . what other soldiers do with their pets if they're not part of a family, or don't have really good friends they can leave their pets with."

"Oh?" his eyebrows raised for a second, his brown eyes squinted just a little. "Well, it's a problem for a few soldiers. I've heard of guys who leave their dog with friends, and the friends don't want to give the dog back. Or the dog runs off, or the friends don't have the time to give the dog proper care.

"Cats are an even harder problem to find homes for, I've heard. There are lots of problems with cats. It's better if the pet goes to a shelter where it will get a new home."

"But don't most shelters have to put most of the animals down?"

"Well, we have to hope that won't happen," he leaned forward in his chair, his manner suddenly serious. "What's bothering you, Cathy? What are you thinking?"

"I don't know," I tried to smile, knowing that tears were suddenly close.

"I was walking with Moose the other day. Chase loved that dog. And I started wondering what he would have done with Moose . . . ."

". . . if you hadn't been there to keep him?"

"Yeah," I shrugged my shoulders, "It's not really a problem of mine. It just made me wonder."

John leaned back in his chair and took a deep breath. He looked at me quizzically for a long moment.

"Want to help?" he asked.

"With what?"

"I've got a soldier right now that's trying to find a home for her four-year-old collie. She's in the National Guard. She just never thought when she bought the dog that she'd be deployed for a year or more."

"She doesn't have family?"

"She does. But the people who adopted her as a kid feel they have their hands full with the responsibilities they have with other kids they've taken in. She was looking into boarding the dog, but the cost is prohibitive . . . more than she'd be paid each month."

I was silent, my mind whirling with where our conversation was heading.

"You've got such a big place out there," John continued. "If you could take in an animal or two, it could really help morale."

"I could talk with her," I hesitated just a little. "I don't have much money. She'd have to pay for his food and medical care. He'd have to get along with Moose. But I could do it if . . . if everything fell into place just right."

"Can I give her your number?"

★ ★ ★

Collette McIntyre . . . and the dog's name was Brady. She'd be calling if she still needed a home for the dog. What did I know about collies? Not much. I'd heard that they barked a lot. Collies had a lot of fur. They'd probably take a lot of grooming to keep them looking presentable.

★ ★ ★

A few hours later, as I pulled into my drive, watching for Moose to appear, I could see my four bird poles and bird feeders had been decimated during my absence. Bears. Black bears. They had come looking for food again.

The seven-foot metal bird feeder poles were bent downward like they were made of plastic. Lying on the ground were the remnants of the colorful bird feeders, torn apart, the seed gone.

Grumbling to myself, I picked up the pieces and carried them to the trash barrel. The bears had already ripped apart at least six feeders during the early spring. Even metal feeders weren't safe in the forest.

I wondered if there was a different way to feed birds. I could scatter the seed on the ground, but that would make the birds more vulnerable to cats and other predators. I took a deep breath and blew it out slowly, trying to stop the churning in my mind. Nothing was ever simple, not even feeding wild birds.

The Department of Natural Resources recommended not feeding birds in this area, but I liked feeding them. I felt peaceful, even hopeful for the world, watching the birds feeding. There were so many different colors and sizes of birds with such curious behaviors. They were cheerful, spunky little creatures.

I had watched one tiny chickadee hanging onto a bird feeder perch in the middle of a rain storm. The wind was blowing the feeder straight out, so that it was perpendicular to the ground and shaking in the air gusts that were buffeting it. The rain was pelting down so hard it was almost hard to see through it. But that wee bird just stuck to the side of the feeder and ate its fill.

The tiny chipmunks got into the act too. They were noisier than the birds with their constant chirping, but they cleaned up the fallen seeds rather nicely. I enjoyed watching them eat. Their tiny cheeks would pouf out like balloons as they stuffed seeds into their faces to carry back to their underground nests.

"The bears got to you too, huh?" Wade Melchor, my neighbor from down the road had come up silently behind me. Tall and gaunt in stature, he had long, thin, blond hair that fell below his shoulders. Every time I saw him, I wanted to tell him his hair needed washing, but so far I had kept my silence.

"They were at your place, too?" I questioned.

"All up and down the road," Wade stated flatly. "They got to everybody. Terry thinks a couple of his cats are missing."

"That's too bad. He dotes on those cats."

"So do bears. They love 'em. I've talked with the DNR. If we can trap any bears, they'll move them somewhere else."

"Trap them! How are you going to do that?" The idea of trapping an animal as big and dangerous as a black bear astonished me.

"A few of us guys are going to dig a pit and bait it," his gray eyes squinted in the sun. "There's just too many of those suckers around here. We got to move 'em out. Too bad we can't just shoot a few."

"That's got to be an awfully big, deep pit. I hear bears can climb like anything."

Wade thrust his shoulders back, sticking his chest out defiantly.

"We know what we're doing. We've pitted bears before."

I didn't respond. I didn't really believe him. Gossip was that he was often drunk or high on coke and maybe other drugs.

I dumped the last of the broken bird feeder parts into the trash barrel and turned back to him, but he was already half way down the drive toward the street. He was leaving as silently as he had arrived. I felt relieved.

★   ★   ★

Collette called just after dinner, and we arranged to meet at my home the next day. I spent the evening reading about collies and wondering how the two dogs would get along.

The more I thought about taking in a soldier's dog, the better I felt about it. In his Will, Chase had left specific, personal treasures to his parents and a few friends. Everything else he had in this world he left to me, with the stipulation that his life insurance pay off our home. This would be a chance to do something with our farm that would benefit a cause that Chase believed in.

At least, I assumed he believed in the war in Iraq. Or was his enlisting just a way to stay proud of his ability to provide for himself? Everything had happened so fast that we hadn't talked enough for me to be sure. But I was positive that if he had been able to find adequate work, he would not have left college until he had his degree.

I knew I didn't want our troops in Iraq. I thought we had our hands full fighting the war in Afghanistan. I didn't understand the need for the war or believe that we were protecting the Iraqi people from harm. It seemed to me that thousands of them were dying, and the country was suffering from terrible hardships because of the war. I wondered if these citizens really wanted our help. It was hard to tell what the truth was and what was media or political spin.

It seemed to me that many countries had murderous tyrants for leaders. Why were we so bent on "saving" Iraq but not in helping the citizens of these other countries? Not that I thought we should be intervening in the other countries either.

It wasn't something I needed to solve or could solve, I reminded myself. "Wiser heads—," as my mother would have said. I couldn't stop the war. But perhaps I could help some of the soldiers. Chase would have believed in that.

★ ★ ★

Collette and Brady pulled into my driveway in a green Taurus station wagon that looked like it had seen much better days. Brady could be seen riding shotgun, sitting in the middle of the passenger seat with his back straight and looking around expectantly. Collette parked her wagon next to my car, reached over to her dog and rubbed the back of his head.

I could imagine her talking to him and telling him that everything was going to be ok.

Leaving Moose in the house, I walked out to meet them.

Collette looked about ten years older than me. She was straight and lean with short-cropped, curly, ash brown hair. Her eyes were so blue they were startling. A loose-fitting, yellow tee shirt hung over the top of stonewashed blue jeans. White walking shoes and a blue denim, ruched shoulder bag completed her very casual ensemble.

Brady had bounded out of the wagon after her, looking alert and very interested in these new surroundings. He was a sable-colored, rough collie with a wide, white collar. His face was a light sable with a streak of white up his long muzzle. His prick ears were rimmed with very dark, sable fur.

When he saw me, he started pulling Collette toward me, straining at the leash until he looked like he would choke.

"He's very sociable," she said, laughing.

"I can see that," I reached out to the dog, and he dove into my hands with a friendly abandon.

Brady bounced quickly around me with an intense curiosity, sniffing my feet and clothes. Abruptly he stood stiffly at attention, one front foot in the air, looking at Moose in the doorway.

"He sees your dog," Collette observed. "I hope they like each other."

"Moose has never been aggressive with people or other dogs," I shared, not mentioning what I knew he would do to a rabbit or raccoon. "Let's go to the back yard where they have some room to get acquainted, and we'll have some control."

"Brady is neutered," Collette said thoughtfully, "but I don't know if that affects the need dogs have for dominance."

"We're about to find out."

I reached for the gate just as Moose arrived on the other side.

Both dogs began barking and whining, jumping against the gate and straining to smell each other through the fence.

Collette looked pensively at Moose.

"He's such a big dog. That worries me a little. Is he easily controlled?"

"He's independent at times, but he wants to mind. He's been lonesome for someone to play with since Chase's been gone. I'm not a rough and tumble kind of person. I'll walk him . . . throw a stick for him, but that's about it."

Collette nodded, watching the dogs closely as the gate opened. Moose and Brady circled each other, sniffing each other carefully.

Brady was the first to break away. He began running in little circles, then bouncing toward Moose, rear end in the air, his front legs on the ground, his head twisting in little excited movements.

Moose glanced at me for just a second before joining in the fun. The dogs tussled in a friendly kind of horseplay and chased each other energetically around the yard. As we watched, they finally started quietly exploring the yard together.

"I think they're going to be friends," I shared, leading the way to some lawn chairs. "Thank God."

Collette nodded.

"I can breathe again," she said, sitting down.

As the dogs played and explored, we sat in the afternoon sunshine and shared the decisions that had brought us to this moment. Collette agreed to send money monthly for Brady's care. Handing me his medical records, she shared that she had found him in a shelter about fifty miles away.

"He was treated badly by his owners as a pup," she explained.

They had kept him isolated, chained alone at a dog house with inadequate food or water. When he was a year old, the sheriff had finally taken him away, malnourished and frightened. Brady had no social skills, having only rare contact with people, and no obedience training.

"I've poured my life into turning that dog around," Collette stated. "I can't believe that I have to leave him. We've been inseparable since I got him. I just don't know how he'll adjust to living without me. I'm afraid he'll have separation anxiety and be a real nuisance. I hope you'll have patience with him."

"I will," I promised. "But I've been thinking . . . it might be a good idea for you to bring him back tomorrow for a few hours. Maybe you could leave him overnight the next day and take him home again. If you do that a few times, he should feel comfortable here, knowing that you will come back for him."

Collette nodded in agreement, her eyes suddenly glistening with tears.

"My life was going so well . . . my job . . . my home. I have to just close it up. Brady's been so excited about his life lately. Now I'm going to abandon him."

She stopped suddenly and looked at her hands.

"Cathy, if I don't come back, what will you do with him?"

My heart felt like it stopped, and tears welled up in my own eyes. I shook my head, unable to speak for a moment.

"Don't even think that way," I begged.

"Can you just keep him?" she asked, looking past me at the playing dogs.

"Sure," I said quickly. "He's safe here forever, if need be. Don't worry about him."

Moose seemed confused when Brady left a short while later. Throughout the evening, he stared at me, seemingly trying to make sense of Brady's visit.

Ten days later, when Brady joined our home for the duration of Collette's tour, he had stayed with us several nights without incident. He was always excited to see Collette when she appeared and happy to leave with her, but more and more confident when she left without him.

As she left for the last time, Brady and Moose stood together at the fence, calm and curious, watching her climb into her station wagon.

She waved to them and then to me, and backed out of the drive.

3

Double Trouble

Brady settled in nicely after Collette left. He lived with expectant hope shining in his eyes and an avid curiosity in everything around him. The scars from his first year of life didn't seem to stop him from enjoying his present life. However, it did affect his personality.

In those rare situations where Moose needed discipline, Brady would quietly slink out the doggy door acting as if the blame had to rest with him. He was an apologetic dog, needing approval, never quite sure if he'd done the right thing. Moose, on the other hand, couldn't believe that he could do anything wrong and was quite shocked when he was scolded.

I left them alone several times for brief periods over the next several days. I finally decided they wouldn't fight with each other or tear up the house if I was gone for several hours. That was a mistake.

Upon my return, I opened the door to be greeted by howls of delight and excited, squirming bodies pressing against my legs. A thin pathway of white fluttery stuff that looked like snow spread across the carpet they were dancing on. I followed them down this trail, noting that the white stuff was getting thicker as we went down the hallway toward the bedroom.

Moose and Brady bounced into my room before I could get there, and white stuff floated up from the floor into the air from huge piles in the doorway and beyond.

Feathers. Thousands of white feathers covered my bed and floor in thick piles. Torn-up pillow cases lay nearby. It was clear they had had a pillow fight. It was also clear they had really loved it. In fact, they were still having a pillow fight, delightedly romping back and forth through the feathers, scattering them into the air to fall wherever.

I should have been mad, or at least upset. But they were so happy, I had trouble finding words to scold them.

It was a tough night. Cleaning up took hours and piles of feathers landed in the front yard.

"The birds are going to have warm nests this year," I thought wryly, as I dumped yet another load of feathers on the front lawn. What I didn't know was that I would be finding feathers throughout the house for years to come.

Both dogs spent the night outdoors with the doggy door locked tight. There was noisy scratching at the door during the night and considerable plaintive barking and whining. Determinedly, I set my heart on hard and went to sleep in the wee hours of the morning when most of the feathers had been cleaned up.

★ ★ ★

Morning dawned much too soon. I went about opening the house up for the day with aching muscles and a groggy mind. As I pulled the blinds open in the living room, I saw Wade Melchor stomping up my driveway.

His shoulders seemed wider than I had ever seen them. Arms swinging, his elbows stuck out on either side of him. His fists were clenched. His jaw set hard. His long, stringy hair was flying behind him. He was taking huge strides with such visible anger that his heels seemed to be burning holes in the dirt drive.

My immediate inclination was to slam the blinds shut and hide.

He saw me in the window and shook his fist at me. His face contorted in anger, and he started yelling something I couldn't understand. My spine felt like it was going to melt, but I walked slowly to the front door and opened it.

The locked screen door did not feel like enough protection, but it was all I had. Moose and Brady were right there with me, I reasoned. He'd have to fight all three of us.

But Brady disappeared as soon as the door opened, and he saw the raging man outside.

Moose, ever the protector, found a safe spot behind me. I could feel his warm body tight against the back of my legs.

"I'm going to kill that dog of yours," Wade shouted, pointing at Moose. "If I ever see him out again, he's dead."

"What did he do?" I asked defensively. "He's been right here all night."

"Oh, no, he hasn't," Wade yelled back. "I've got pictures of him. And it's him all right!"

"What did he do?" I asked again, less defensively.

"He's been robbing the bear bait, that's what he's been doing."

"The what?"

"The bear bait!" he fairly screamed, his raging face close to the screen.

I looked at him, not comprehending, my face a study in confusion. He threw up his hands and took a step away from the door. Grabbing his head with both hands, his lanky body twisted in circles for a minute.

"Arghhh," he growled. And I could hear him thinking, "city woman."

"The bear bait," he said sweetly, enunciating the words slowly through clenched teeth. "It took the guys days to dig that blasted pit big enough to hold a bear. We covered it with branches. Just the right size of branches so they'd break under the bear's weight and drop him in the hole. To be sure he went on the branches, we put a nice roast of venison in the middle of it. That is called bear bait!"

"Oh," I said, feeling stupid. "I understand."

"Well," he continued with feigned courtesy, "the bait has been disappearing. We put it out and every morning it's gone. Five days now. Last night we staked it out to see what was getting the bait but not breaking the branches. And it's your dang dog!" he fairly shrieked.

"I'm sorry. I don't know what else to say."

I looked down at Moose who was watching the scene with large, curious eyes.

"I don't know how he was getting out. The fence was locked."

"He jumps the fence!" Wade looked at me as if I were being deliberately dense. "That four foot fence isn't high enough to stop a dog like him."

"I'm sorry," I said again. "I thought he'd stopped jumping when he put on some extra pounds. I'll try to fix it right away."

He pinched his lips tightly together, stopping himself from saying what was about to burst out of them. He turned on his heel and stomped down the drive.

Moose raced outdoors. From behind the protection of the fence, he barked fiercely at Wade's departing back.

★   ★   ★

For a week after that, I locked both dogs in the kitchen when I left the house. They had access to the doggy door and their water bowl from the kitchen.

"Dogs are pack animals," I reasoned. "Being isolated away from me, the home, and comforts they were used to enjoying should be punishment for them. They'll learn not to damage things."

At least that was the message I hoped they'd get.

When I would come home, I kept them with me in the kitchen. But I didn't praise or pet them until I had examined the kitchen carefully. Together we checked the table and chairs, the woodwork, and the cabinets. I even examined the plant on the counter.

I looked around every area of the floor, occasionally looking directly into their eyes and asking questions about the condition of the kitchen. They would both stand very close to me, curiously trying to watch everything I was doing.

When it was clear that the kitchen was in good order, I would praise and pet them. Then I would open the door to the rest of the house.

I hoped this would teach them to stop damaging the house. I knew I should know more about dog behavior than I did, and I promised myself to get a dog training book the next time I was in Traverse City. In the meantime, I hoped they would learn there would be consequences if they misbehaved.

It almost worked.

After a week, I left them in the house alone and went for a long ride. The house was intact when I returned. I felt reassured. But two days later, when I went shopping, I returned to another disaster.

I opened the door to find they had torn an overstuffed chair apart. Stuffing and pieces of wood lay scattered about the living room floor. Upholstery material used for a tug of war was stretched, ripped, and strewn about the room. I sat down in the midst of the mess and had a frustrated, angry cry.

Moose and Brady hovered around me, obviously concerned at the strange noises I was making and my apparent distress.

In a few minutes, still without speaking to them and still sniffing, I leashed both dogs. I put the handle of their leashes around my arm, forcing them to trot along with me as I cleaned up. I put the pieces of wood in the seat of the chair and the foam and upholstery material in a large plastic bag. They hiked along and watched as I put the plastic bag in the big trash pickup can. I left them in the house while I dragged what was left of the chair outside to the trash pickup area.

They were watching through the screen door when I returned. I walked them to the kitchen and shut them in for the night. I didn't pet them. I didn't talk to them. I didn't feed them. I locked the doggy door so they couldn't go outside. Then I went to my bedroom and crashed.

In the morning, I opened the doggy door and let them outside. I put out food for them, locked the kitchen door and left for the day. I still hadn't petted or spoken to them. They silently watched me through the fence as I drove away.

It was another week of kitchen lockdown before I let them into the rest of the house. They were subdued dogs that slunk into my bedroom that night and found places to sleep. But it was the end of damage to my home or belongings.

Something had clicked in their minds. They treated me and my home with respect from that day forward.

4

Bear Corridor

One thing about having two large dogs, I discovered, was the need for daily back yard cleanup. With just Moose, I was often able to let it go a day or two but not with the two of them.

Chase and I had fenced in about two-thirds of an acre of land in back of the house. Some of it was wooded, but most of it Chase had leveled and seeded with grass.

I had intended to plant some rose bushes, to make a small garden with greens, tomatoes, and herbs, but I didn't get it done while I was working, and with Chase gone, I didn't have the heart for it.

Now trotting around the area looking for dog piles every day was a half-hour of exercise I often begrudged.

I was pacing about the yard, scoop and bag in hand, when I heard a car coming up the drive. Both dogs were already at the fence, excitedly craning their necks to see who was there. I knew the barking would start as soon as the car door opened.

As I came around the side of my house to the front, John Dunnom was ringing my door bell, and the dogs were already inside the house barking at him through an open window.

"Good morning, John," I called to him, unaware at first that he had another man with him. "Stopping by for coffee?"

"Sounds good, Cathy. I wanted you to meet Rob Brimley," he gestured toward the sandy-haired, good-looking man who had been standing beside him.

"Rob, this is Cathy Maslin," he stepped aside, and Rob held out his hand.

I knew without being told that he was Army. I noted that he had a firm, friendly grip as we shook hands. I liked his smile immediately, but his brown eyes seemed very reserved, almost cold. Unusual for brown eyes, I thought. They were usually friendly, warm eyes.

"We'll need to go in the back door," I gestured toward the back yard. "I hope you're used to big dogs."

Moose and Brady were back at the fence as we went back through the gate. John closed the gate behind us as the dogs bounced around, looking for attention.

"How is Brady doing?" he asked pleasantly. "He's looking good."

"He seems to be doing fine," I answered. "Moose and Brady like each other a lot. At first, they got into more mischief than I want to think about, but they've calmed down."

As I set coffee and donuts on the table, I described the pillow fight they had had and watched the men chuckling. I saw John looking around my kitchen, and I looked too.

I hadn't thought of looking at my house critically for some time. My dishes carried a blue floral motif that didn't look like any flower that I had ever seen, but they seemed to have a joy about them. Over the stainless steel sink was a double window that looked into the back yard. The window curtains were white, trimmed with a wide, blue-checkered edging. The floor was a multi-toned beige tile that blended well with the oak-colored cabinets that marched around the room. Where wall space was visible, we had painted it a soft blue to match the fake marble counters that the salesman had promised would wear even better than real marble.

"It's been a while since you've been in this kitchen," I remarked quietly.

"It has," John nodded. "Looks just the same as the last time I was here. Sure brings back memories. Good memories." He hastened to add.

I smiled and nodded.

We were silent for a moment, lost in our own thoughts, drinking our coffee.

Rob was the first to speak.

"John told me about your taking in the collie for a National Guardsman."

"Yes," I nodded. "Brady's a sweet dog. I have the feeling you're also in the Army."

It was his turn to nod.

"Yes," he shared. "I've been in for eleven years. I've been home for a few weeks now. I'll need to go back soon."

"And I'll just bet you have a dog and no one to look after him," I glanced at John and then back to Rob who returned my gaze with amused eyes.

"And you would be a mind reader," he grinned. "Yes, I have a dog. She's nine years old, a Shepherd-mix, nowhere near the size of these guys."

He gestured toward Moose and Brady who were lying together at my feet, pretending to sleep, but with a watchful eye on the food.

"I thought it was a good idea to bring Rob out so you two could talk," John intervened. "If you don't want another dog, just say so. We'll understand."

"I guess I'm wondering why, after nine years, you need someone to take care of her. How have you been managing up to now?"

"She's my mother's dog," Rob explained. "But Mom's had a stroke. She's in a nursing home. We're hoping she may get better in time, but for right now she can't take care of herself, let alone a dog."

"Oh, that's tough," I frowned. "You must be worried about her."

"I am, but she's past the worst of it now. She could recover enough, in time, to go home. I'd really hate for Mom to find out that we put her dog down because she wasn't able to care for it for a few months."

"That really could upset her," I agreed.

"She's getting good care, and my sister is nearby. She'd look after Daisy, but her kids are allergic to dogs," he paused and then added, "And her husband isn't fond of Daisy at all."

"Why not?" I asked, suddenly on the alert. "Does she bite?"

"No. Well, of course she could bite if she felt the need, but I've never known her to bite," Rob tried to explain. "She's too noisy for him, I think."

"Noisy?"

"She's got a really loud bark," Rob said, emphasizing each word carefully and looking directly into my eyes. "She really does."

"Well, I can't imagine that would be a bother out here in the woods. It might even help keep the bears away. I guess we'd have to see," I glanced away briefly. "These dogs are both neutered. Is Daisy?"

Rob nodded, his eyes watching me closely.

He had a healthy, physical kind of male good looks that weren't lost on me. I could imagine myself feeling a little dizzy. I looked at John. No relief there. Pensively, I traced the rim of my coffee cup with my finger and tried to think.

"I've been alone too much," I thought suddenly. "These guys could talk me into taking five dogs."

"Is Daisy with you now?" I heard myself asking.

"She's in the car," Rob admitted.

Daisy was lying on her back in the back seat in a pose I was to learn was her favorite sleeping position. Her head was lying with the side of her face on the seat, her front feet pointed upward, curved downward at the knees. Her back legs were also pointed upward but splayed apart and tipped in the opposite direction to her head. The side of one of her back feet rested against the back of the seat. She looked like a small black and tan Shepherd with the gentle face and head shape of a Labrador Retriever.

"She looks comfortable," I observed, looking in the car window. My voice woke her and Daisy looked into my eyes without moving.

John opened the car door with a grin of agreement, and Rob gave a low "come to me" type whistle.

Daisy rose and stretched, displaying the black saddle marking so typical of shepherds, clearly visible on her back. Her long tail began waving slowly and happily as she jumped from the car. Daisy started to run to Rob but stopped suddenly, staring beyond me.

Only then did I realize that Moose was with us.

"Where did he come from?" John asked.

"He jumps the fence," I explained quickly, reaching for him. Moose eluded me and met Daisy head on. He was at least twice her size.

"He's always been friendly with other dogs," I assured the men, even though I felt a twinge of nervousness.

The dogs circled each other warily, sniffing each other with diligence. Daisy finally stood still, looking toward Rob, and the doggy-style introductions ended. Moose stepped away and looked at me, his eyes questioning.

"Good boy, Moose," I said, glancing back to the fence where Brady was watching us, barking plaintively.

As we turned to walk to the back yard, Daisy took the lead, her little feet dancing rapidly across the ground, her black and beige tail floating, waving, above her back. Moose followed, watching her intently.

Brady made Moose look like the soul of restraint. He danced around on his hind feet as the dogs approached the fence and met Daisy with shrill barks, whirling smartly around her. Daisy jumped at him, too, as they went through the sniffing ritual, and then Daisy raced around the yard with Brady in hot pursuit.

Moose continued to stand and watch, his expression pensive, his straight, black tail moving slowly to and fro. As Daisy and Brady shot past us, Moose joined the chase, and the three of them tore around the yard again.

Daisy turned suddenly, ran toward Rob and collapsed at his feet, panting. Brady and Moose stopped running immediately and sat down nearby, watching us with heads up, eyes shining, and tongues hanging.

"They're getting along, right?" I asked the men, laughing.

"I'd say so," Rob replied, adding. "Daisy and Brady are both herding dogs so they'll have a lot in common."

"Plus she's a female," John inserted.

"So she's just given them something to think about," Rob laughed.

"She could be the new alpha dog in this pack," John remarked.

I thought about that. I wasn't sure I wanted Moose replaced as top dog in the house. Somehow I'd thought since it was his house, he would be the leader of any dogs that joined us. Maybe that wouldn't be true.

"Has Brady ever jumped the fence?" John asked suddenly.

"No," I said quickly. "Brady hasn't challenged the fence at all, but Moose is a problem."

As we watched the dogs playing together, I told them about Wade's visit and his threats.

"I priced fencing," I continued. "I can pay for the materials, but finding someone to put it in is a problem. I'm told it will be weeks before anyone has time, and then it will cost a fortune."

Shaking my head ruefully, I gestured helplessly with one hand.

"I'm afraid it would take me the rest of my life to do it myself."

"We could probably get some buddies together and do it," Rob spoke thoughtfully. "Don't count on it yet, we'd have to talk to some people. But assuming that we can pull it off, I would think you'd want some runs for dogs as well as a large open area. Right?"

"I hadn't thought about runs," I said slowly. "But if several dogs are here, it would be a good idea. There might be a time when they'd need to be separated."

"Let's take a closer look at your yard so I'll know what I'm talking about," Rob suggested.

With the dogs exploring around us, we discussed how the house was positioned with the area already fenced and what kind of fencing would be most helpful to restrain dogs. John suggested placing the runs against the barn so that I could have indoor shelter for dogs too. I liked the idea and so did Rob.

At one corner of the fenced area near the house was a small area of at least a hundred Jack Pines growing closely together. Growing about forty feet high, many of the trees had been pruned just high enough to walk under their scraggly branches. The upper branches of the Jack Pines had woven together as they grew, forming a canopy over the entire area. These trees had laid a soft, scented carpet of pine needles on the ground for many years.

It was a place that the dogs particularly liked, perhaps because of the shade and the softness of the ground. It was also a nesting place for many birds. I could always see Moose, and now Brady, in this corner watching me as I drove away from home.

Walking under the trees, the soft needles underfoot, the world seemed very far away. I felt peaceful and relaxed. The men had stopped talking and seemed to be absorbing the tranquil mood of this wooded place.

John was the first to break the silence.

"A dog should be happy out here."

"I love it and I think they do too," I agreed. "There's serenity in the forest. I think it's deeply healing to a person—or a dog."

"Whoa," Rob said quietly, "that's a bear." He gestured toward the back fence where a large, black bear was undulating over the fence like a child's toy slinky.

The bear took a couple of tentative steps into the yard, looking around, then backed to the fence and slid over it out of the yard. He took a few steps into the woods, turned, and came back to the fence. He rose up a little on his hind feet, sniffing the air, settled down on all fours, and took another step, still undecided.

"That's a really big bear," Rob stated, moving silently on the pine needles for a closer look. "I don't think he's seen us."

"He smells food, I'll bet," John said quietly. "What can we use to make some noise?"

"The rocks out here are so small," I answered. "I doubt they'd be loud enough to scare him."

The bear undulated back over the fence, hesitated only a moment longer, and then walked determinedly into the yard toward a bird feeder I had forgotten was there.

Brady suddenly appeared from the side of the house, trotting out to meet the newcomer. His tail was up, his manner friendly.

"Oh, no," I whispered, wanting to scream. Rob grabbed my arm and pulled me back as I instinctively took a shaky step forward.

The bear saw Brady and turned toward him with a growl we could hear in the Jack Pines. He ran hard at Brady, who turned quickly and ran for the house.

Then everything happened so fast that I could barely comprehend it all.

Moose, running hard toward them, cut between Brady and the bear. Brady whirled around, barking shrilly, and started back toward the bear when he saw Moose run behind him.

Daisy let out the loudest bark I had ever heard in a dog and shot out of the Jack Pines toward the bear. Racing forward, she barked fiercely with every step.

Moose reached the bear first. The huge animal rose up on his hind feet and swatted at Moose with both front paws. Moose spun in the air, landing on his side. He jumped up instantly, and started back toward the bear, just as Daisy hurled into the scene.

Faced with the three dogs, the bear turned, made a fast exit over the fence, and disappeared into the woods.

My heart was thundering in my ears as I found myself stumbling from the safety of the pines. The men, sprinting toward the dogs, were halfway across the yard in a heartbeat, and I raced to keep up.

The dogs, spinning excitedly, were lined up at the fence barking wildly at the departing bear. The agitated dogs rushed at us as we approached, circling us in a frenzy, still barking fiercely.

I tried to pull Moose into my arms to see if he was injured, but he was too excited to hold still and kept struggling to watch the bear's retreat. Brady wanted petting and lots of it. John rubbed Brady hard as he tried to get a look at Moose. Daisy, her legs flashing as she dashed about, finally leapt into Rob's arms.

"His eye looks squashed," John pointed out. "We'd best get him to a vet."

My heart sank as I saw that the flesh around Moose's eye was hanging loosely an inch down his cheek, exposing the inside of his lower lid. Although the flesh was blood red and wet appearing, it didn't seem to be bleeding. But his eye seemed to be sunk into his head. As Moose strained to watch the bear, I could see that the white of his eye was blood red also.

As we left the yard, John grabbed the troublesome bird feeder, and hung it on a shepherd's hook in the front yard as he passed.

We took all the dogs with us to the vet. Daisy and Brady rode with John in his car. Rob put Moose in the back of my car and rode with me.

By the time we got to Dr. Barett's Veterinary Clinic, Moose was lying quietly in the back seat. He acted exhausted. I was frantic, fighting tears.

"He'll be fine," Rob said reassuringly, "just take it easy."

"I've never seen a bear in the back yard before," I shared, biting my lip. "Never. I was sure they'd never climb the fence so close to the house."

"How about the front yard?" he asked.

"All the time," I replied. "We're in a bear corridor through the forests, according to the DNR. We didn't know that when we bought the place. I found that out after Chase left. I guess we should have known. You can't live in a forest without wild animals around."

"Comes with the territory," he smiled.

★ ★ ★

Dr. Barett was examining Moose's eye when I pointed out, with surprise, that a few drops of blood had fallen from his tail to the examining table. Dr. Barett let go of Moose's face and turned his attention to his tail. As he lifted it up, a long gaping wound appeared. Moose's tail was slit open from the tip of the tail to his bottom.

"That's his artery," Dr. Barett pointed to a long vessel that hung loosely the length of the slit when he lifted his tail.

"If he'd touched that on anything rough, a bush, a tough weed, if the bear's nail had gone in a fraction further, he'd have died before he could have gotten to the house. Even in the car . . . ," he stopped talking and shook his head.

Dr. Barett drew a step back and looked at Moose, then at me.

"I've got to use an anesthetic," he said. "He's going to need a lot of stitches to close that up. His eye should be all right. The flesh will tighten up again, and there doesn't appear to be any permanent damage to the eyeball itself. It looks like some broken blood vessels. I'll check it out closer while he's under. He'll need to recover from surgery tonight. You can pick him up tomorrow afternoon."

He gave me a little hug as I left.

"He'll be good as new in a few days," he said gently.

I hugged him back. Dr. Barett was elderly. He could have retired years earlier, but loved the animals and his practice. His skinny torso felt old, his white hair looked old, but his blue eyes spoke of an energetic spirit, a crackerjack mind and a robust sense of humor. I had loved him on sight and my feelings for him hadn't diminished as I got to know him better.

He was a kindly man with an indomitable spirit. He cared for Moose the way he would have cared for his own dog. He cared for his animal client's guardians too. He understood the deep affection that exists between a pet and its people and did what he could to assuage their anxiety in times of crisis.

Now was just such a time.

Outside in the cool, spring air, I felt the anxiety slipping away. Moose was going to be all right. Brady and Daisy hadn't been hurt. I leaned against the side of my car and took a deep breath. John reached for the door handle of my car as Rob stood supportively close to me.

"Thanks for coming with me," I said slowly. "It helped to have you here."

"Glad to do it," John said quickly. "Are you going to be all right? Have the bears ever been threatening before?"

"No. No, they haven't. They just clean out the bird feeders. I've never really worried about them before."

"Those dogs made quite a fighting unit," Rob remarked, "considering they were new to each other and all."

"I noticed that too," I looked at him. "Do you still want to leave Daisy with me, or will you worry about her with all the wild creatures out there?"

"I think she'll be fine with you," Rob said, smiling. "I'll take her home with me tonight, but I'll bring her back before I leave."

Brady went home with me, riding in the front passenger seat, his back straight, his eyes curious and watchful, just as he had ridden with Collette. I realized suddenly that I was becoming very fond of him. It was going to be hard to part with him when she returned.

During the evening, he seemed a little puzzled but very pleased to be the only dog in the house. When I woke in the early hours of the morning, I found him stretched out beside me on the bed, something he had never done before.

When I moved, he opened his eyes but held very still. I could feel the tension suddenly flowing through him. I reached over and stroked his silky head, to which he responded by stretching lazily and closing his eyes. I wondered about my commitment to take in these dogs. Parting was going to be very hard.

5

The Face Of Anger

Thanks to the antibiotics he had to take, Moose slept a lot for the next few days. Both he and Brady checked his tail periodically. I had expected that he would scratch or bite at the thirty-three stitches it had taken to sew his tail together, but he didn't.

"He's one lucky dog," Dr. Barett had said when I picked him up. "All the meat that should have protected the artery was shoved into the flesh just above his butt. That bear really got him."

"It happened so fast," I told him.

"His eyes will be ok in a few days," Dr. Barett continued. "I'd be careful to keep the dogs away from the bears out there in the future."

"He jumps the fence," I shared. "Controlling him is easier said than done."

"And you're taking in more dogs?"

"Well, a couple, maybe."

"A couple so far," he smiled at me kindly, "but with the plan you've outlined to me, there may be more in the future. I'm thinking you could use some help learning more about dogs, Cathy."

I nodded. He was very right and I knew it.

"I know a man in town, Tom Ingalls. He's an engineer, but he's also an expert dog handler. He was training dogs as an avocation before going in the Army. He's been back a while and hasn't really gotten settled at anything yet. I could ask him to call you."

"I'd like that," I nodded. "I could use some help."

★ ★ ★

There was no word from Rob over the next several days. I had about decided that he had been scared off by the bear when John called one morning.

"Cathy," he said, "Rob was called back to duty suddenly. He brought Daisy to me late last night. Can I bring her out this evening, or can you come and get her? It's hard for me to get off duty today."

★ ★ ★

When I arrived a few hours later, I found that John had Daisy leashed and tied to the leg of his desk. She remembered me immediately and got up to meet me, her tail wagging, her eyes bright and questioning.

"She's so quiet," I observed and heard John laugh.

"She's the loudest dog I've ever heard," he said. "I would have kept her a couple of days, but an hour after Rob dropped her off with me, my neighbors were threatening to sign a petition."

"That bad, huh?" I looked at Daisy sitting quietly at the foot of the desk, not quite believing him. "Why did Rob have to leave so fast? Don't they usually have a little notice?"

"He's Special Forces, Cathy," John said quietly. "They're lucky to get any notice sometimes. Yesterday, he got an order to report to his base immediately. He'll call you when he gets a minute."

"So that's why his eyes are so hard!" I heard myself blurting out, and added quickly, "I'm sorry, I shouldn't have said that. His eyes just didn't seem to match the rest of him."

"He's seen too much," John shared. "He's been in a long time. But no one comes back the same person they were when they shipped out."

I looked sharply at him. He was saying that Chase would have changed, that he wouldn't have been the same man he was when he left. I didn't want to believe that. I wanted to remember Chase as I had known him.

"I think we've almost got a team together to build a better fence for you," I heard John saying.

"OK," I nodded, stroking Daisy's head. "That will be a big help. Let me know what I need to do." I rose quickly, smiling at him. I just wanted to leave.

He took an envelope from his desk, untied Daisy and handed the envelope and her leash to me. His movements were deliberate and unhurried, and I wanted to scream at him to hurry up. My insides had started churning with a strange feeling akin to anxiety, and I felt a desperate need for privacy.

"It's from Rob," John said. "I think it's some money and her health records."

"OK," I nodded, a numb smile on my lips, and headed for the door. "Thanks, John."

I didn't go home. I was too upset to drive far. The beach beckoned, and I stopped there, hungry for the physical release that would come with a long walk.

Daisy seemed to know that I wasn't in the best of moods. She trotted along beside me as if she had gone for walks with me a hundred times. She didn't bark or chase the birds strutting on the beach, for which I was grateful.

The sun was high, warm, and bright in an almost cloudless sky. The lake shimmered under the sun's rays, turning the water a light silver blue. Pools and streaks of water in a deep, Mediterranean blue peppered the silver blue bay.

We passed several white swans in the shallow areas, with a few black swans gliding lazily among them. The swans drifted majestically among dozens of ducks cruising busily in the bay, many of them flipping head down into the water after some luckless fish. Even more ducks, mostly mallards, the males resplendent with their bright green neck bands, padded about the beach sands.

A few people were walking on the beach, but no one was swimming in the still frigid water. Sailboats were in abundance against the horizon, their colorful sails stiff against the lake breeze.

The tranquil scenes seemed to bounce off my eyes like a still life painting, unable to draw me into their physical presence, unable to enter my spirit, or thaw the frozen feelings sitting like a rock in my chest.

About a mile down the coast, I found a bench and sat down. Another group of swans, beautiful white swans, about eight of them, large and graceful, were floating in the Bay. The contrast between their delicate, peaceful beauty and my tumultuous feelings deepened and melted the pain in my heart. I wanted desperately to cry.

Chase seemed so far away. I didn't want to think that he would have changed, that our lives would never have been what we had planned. But I had seen change in him when he had come home from Boot camp. He was more assertive, stronger physically, and more restless than I had ever known him to be. I had been proud of him, but my heart had remained frightened at the risk he was taking.

I knew John was right. No one could go into a shooting war, seeing other soldiers maimed and killed, civilians and towns destroyed, and all the hurt and pain that went with such scenes and not be affected.

I wanted, needed, to blame someone, anyone, for everything that had happened. I just didn't know who to blame: the Iraqis for putting up with a tyrant dictator until they needed to be rescued; the President for starting a war with someone who had not declared war on us; big business for taking its work to other countries where labor was cheaper; everyone for their particular form of greed and ignorance that had put the nation into an economic decline; the

Army for not protecting its troops better; John for talking Chase into enlisting?

God help me, maybe I was even angry at Chase. Why did he enlist? Why did he go? Why couldn't he have trusted that the economy would get better?

Why didn't he just take out another school loan and keep on working on his degree? I felt abandoned by him.

Yes, I was angry with him, and I didn't want to be. Anyone else . . . I could be angry with anyone else but not Chase. But I was angry with him. I could feel a helpless rage born of confusion and loss tearing at my heart.

"Why? Why? Why had he enlisted?" I asked myself. "Why couldn't he have believed we'd make it as a team even if it was hard? What made him so proud he had to take such a risk?"

I knew it was a guy thing, but that didn't help.

The tears began to flow, slowly at first and then deeply, stopping my breath, causing me to choke and sob. I fumbled in my purse for a tissue and became aware that Daisy, Sweet Daisy, had been licking my fingers, apparently trying to comfort me.

As I moved my hand, she began to lick my arm. Her eyes watched me with concern, her tail slowly, hopefully, thumping on the sand. I slid down from the bench onto the beach, cuddled her to me, and let my tears fall softly, quietly, onto her thick fur.

★   ★   ★

"I didn't realize until today that I was angry with Chase," I shared with Bea. "It hit me like a ton of bricks. I'm just . . . I just feel torn apart inside."

Bea looked at me, pursing her full lips. Her blue eyes, red freckles and carrot red hair stood out starkly against her white skin.

"Tell me about it," she said finally, "why are you angry with him?"

I wiped away the tears that were again streaming down my face and tried to collect my thoughts. Bea was my best friend. She had known Chase almost as long as I had. We had gone to school together, worked at the local theatre's candy counter together through high school, double dated together, and when Bea married Jim, I was her maid of honor. She knew me as well as anyone in the world.

She had been thrilled for me when I met Chase, rejoiced with me when we bought the farm, commiserated with me when he joined the Army. She had been my matron of honor at our wedding and grieved with me when he died.

An hour earlier, I had left the beach with Daisy but couldn't bring myself to go home. I didn't want to be alone. I needed company badly. I needed to talk. Bea was the obvious choice.

She had opened her door, taken one look at my tear-stained face, swollen eyes and red nose, and wordlessly pulled me inside. She led me into the kitchen and poured each of us a cup of coffee. Sitting at the kitchen table, where we had spent countless hours of our lives, was comforting in itself.

"Am I ever going to get past this?" I asked, staring into my coffee cup at the black, steaming liquid.

"Every day it's something new. I had no idea I was angry with Chase. I don't want to be angry with him." Tears were flowing again. "How can I be angry with him? I love him. He didn't want to die. He had everything to live for, and so did I."

"Anger doesn't have to be reasonable, Cathy. It's a feeling, and feelings aren't facts. You know that."

"Well, these feelings hurt. They really do hurt. And that's a fact."

"I believe you," Bea said in a strong voice. "I really do believe you."

We were quiet then for what seemed like an eternity. I didn't know what else to say. Daisy sat beside me, her chin on my knee, staring up at me. I stroked her head mindlessly. Bea drank her coffee, waiting, trying not to watch me too closely.

"I just needed to tell someone." The tears were welling up again in my eyes. I took a deep breath and willed them away.

"Sure," Bea nodded encouragingly.

"I guess I'm ok now," I said finally. "I don't know what else to say, and I just feel tired."

Bea reached for my arm and gave it a little squeeze.

"I'm here anytime you want to talk, Cathy, or cry," she said gently. "I wish I could remember where I saw it, but this article said that grief has stages a person has to go through to feel happy again. Anger was one of those stages."

"Sometimes," I said, rising and picking up my purse. "I think I'm going to feel this way forever."

"I'll be out to see you soon," Bea said, giving me a hug as I left. "I want to meet all these dogs you've been accumulating. You'll have a kennel going soon."

6

The Fence

The two white, rattan lawn chairs and a small, rattan table I kept on the front porch were scattered across the front yard when I reached home. Had my house been robbed? Vandalized?

My eyes anxiously searched the back fence for Moose and Brady. I felt a sense of relief when both dogs charged into sight, barking a frantic sounding welcome at the sight of my car. So I probably hadn't been robbed. I couldn't imagine anyone going in the house with both dogs there.

I parked my car, feeling anger surging through my veins. It had to have been Wade, trying to give me a hard time. No one else in the area had ever shown any anger toward me. I couldn't imagine any other neighbor being aggressive enough to throw my furniture off my front porch.

Daisy, her tail waving happily, trotted along with me to pick up the furniture. The chairs were light weight but bulky, awkward to carry, and the rattan had sharp ends sticking out of their weave. I was struggling to half drag, half carry, the chair to the porch when I felt a sharp sting as a bamboo shard scratched my leg.

All the events of the day boiled together, and I felt a fury of anger. I dropped the chair and gave it a solid, satisfying kick.

Seconds later, I heard the gravel of the driveway crunching.

Daisy left me instantly, barking wildly, and raced toward the shiny, black pickup pulling into my yard. I didn't know the driver who had, obviously, from the smirk on his face, seen me kick the chair.

Embarrassed, still angry, knowing I wasn't being reasonable, I decided I didn't like him. Whoever he was, I didn't like him.

As he stepped from the pickup, I could see that he was a pleasant looking man a few years older than me. Tall and slender, he had a rawboned look much like Wade's, which didn't help him much in my eyes. He was wearing relaxed fit blue jeans, a light blue shirt with the sleeves rolled halfway to his elbows. His belt buckle bore a metal cutout of a hunting dog.

Daisy acted like she knew him, standing on her hind legs and bouncing on and off his legs as he walked. He greeted her with a word I couldn't hear, gave her a couple of pats, and continued toward me with a quiet assurance. Daisy followed him with obvious deference.

After a few steps, I saw that he had a barely discernible limp, which didn't seem to affect his pace as he closed the distance between us. His hair was dark ash brown. His eyes were bluish, maybe grayish-green. I couldn't be sure, as he seemed to be squinting a bit. A white, puckered scar ran across the side of his neck and disappeared under his collar. The skin on the back side of the scar was reddish and shiny.

"I'm Tom Ingalls," he said holding out his hand to me, and I saw evidence of the same scarring on his arm. "Some friends of yours have asked me to stop out and see what I could do to help."

"Oh," I reached out to him, feeling a gentle strength as his hand closed over mine, "Dr. Barett. You're his army friend. He said he would call you."

"Right," he politely refrained from staring at my still swollen eyes, "and John told me you needed some fencing work done," he glanced around the yard, noting Moose and Brady in the back yard. "It seems that you've taken on some foster dogs."

"You know John, too?" I questioned, surprised.

"It's a small world," he smiled, "we're both in the same army, from the same town. Did you want some help with these chairs?"

"They belong on the porch."

I started to reach for one, but he waved me off and picked the chair up easily by the back of the seat. As we walked toward the porch, Tom picked the second chair up in his other hand as we passed it.

"They're nice chairs," he commented, looking down at me as I picked up the small table.

"I hope they're not broken," I said, setting the table on the porch. "I just found them out here. Someone apparently threw them off the porch while I was in town."

"Who would do that?" he asked with some curiosity.

"I'm guessing it was Wade, a neighbor who doesn't like my dog. I can't imagine anyone else around here doing something this petty."

"Umm, I think John mentioned him to me. Your dog was stealing his bear bait."

"That's him, and that's my dog," I gestured helplessly toward Moose, standing wide-eyed and curious at the fence. "I don't really know what to do about either one of them."

Tom laughed easily.

"Well, let's meet your dog."

The next hour passed like a few minutes. Tom met Moose and Brady, neither of whom acted like they normally did. They behaved like model dogs doing anything he asked them to do. All three dogs watched him intensely as if they didn't want to miss anything he did.

As we walked about the yard, I told him about Moose's penchant for jumping the fence, hunting and eating wild animals in the area, even those long dead.

"His behavior got worse when Brady joined us," I shared wearily, and described the escalation in destructive behavior that had occurred after Brady came to live with us.

Tom didn't appear even a little overwhelmed by their antics.

"They're good dogs," he said at one point. "They're trainable, smart, and good natured. They may need more direction from you. They need to know what you want, and that you're serious about what you're telling them to give you.

"That's in your tone of voice. Don't scold them. Just be firm. Get their attention and say in a word or two what you want them to do. Once you have their respect and they know you're dependable, they'll come around."

Later, we walked around the yard and the three dogs followed obediently behind us as we discussed the fence and what he could do to replace it. He and John had asked several Army buddies in the area to help build the fence.

"We've had no problem getting men to help when they learn it's Chase's home," Tom explained. "When they learn the fence is to secure an area to protect deployed soldiers' dogs, everyone said they'd help. It shouldn't take long to complete."

When he left, with the promise of returning with a crew the next day, I felt that he had taken over the responsibility for a huge burden of mine. In spite of myself, I liked him. I felt an inner strength in him that was reassuring. We hadn't talked about him at all, but I felt that I knew him. I found myself looking forward to seeing him again.

Once the fence was built, and Moose was confined, perhaps Wade would leave me alone.

"Then again, knowing Wade," I thought ruefully, "he'll probably find something else about me that he doesn't like."

★ ★ ★

Morning dawned with the air glowing with golden rays of sunlight. For the first time in months, I felt hopeful, even excited, about what the day would bring. I fed the dogs and tidied the house quickly. I wanted to be free to help any way I could when Tom and the other men arrived to work on the fence.

In the living room, I dusted the tables quickly and then the mantel over the fireplace, stopping to hold Chase's picture for a precious moment.

"I miss you, Chase," I told the picture, "I think you'd like the changes I'm making. I think you'd like Brady and Daisy. Tom seems like a nice man. John knows him too. We're going to build a fence high enough to keep Moose from jumping over it. I wish you were here. I really need you to be here."

My heart began to ache as I talked to Chase's picture, looking into those intense blue eyes, and I knew the tears would not be far off. It wouldn't be good to be crying when Tom arrived. I put the picture back on the mantel and left the room quickly.

In the sunroom, I glanced out the window toward the driveway. To my shock, the chairs and little table were back in the yard, tumbled about as if thrown there by an uncaring hand.

"Wade! How could he have done this again?" I thought with considerable anger. "Sneaking into my yard during the night and tossing my furniture around like this. What ails the man? Is he crazy?"

I was putting the table back on the porch when Tom arrived with two other men. His pickup was loaded with bags of cement, steel posts and a machine that looked like a small plow.

He looked at the upside down chairs quizzically.

"Again?"

"I'm going to have to talk to Wade," I shook my head in frustration. "This really can't go on."

"When did it happen?"

"I don't know. It was this way when I got up," I answered. "I didn't hear anything. The dogs didn't bark during the night."

"Strange behavior for a grown man," Tom observed. "Sure there are no kids around that might do this?"

"Not close by, except for Wade's kids," I answered tentatively, thinking of where kids or teens in the area lived. "Not close enough to get here at night without a car, that's for sure."

As they put the chairs back on the porch, Tom introduced the men with him. One of them told me that he had known Chase from high school football. I felt a surge of warmth toward Tom and his crew.

"I've got drinks inside, and sandwiches when you get hungry," I told them before I returned to the house.

The chairs replaced, Tom backed his pickup near the back yard fence. His friends unloaded the material, placing bags of cement and a post about every six feet along the old fence. They acted like they had built fences together many times.

Tom had recommended that the new fence be completed a few feet outside the old fence. I agreed. Keeping the old fence intact for a while solved a headache I didn't want to have. I needed a place to keep the dogs while the project was being worked on, which would surely take a few days.

For a few minutes I watched with amusement as all three dogs paced the fence busily and noisily observing the action. Some of the men would stop at times and good-naturedly talk to the dogs for a few seconds before returning to work.

Going into the kitchen, I made a fresh pot of coffee and pitcher of iced tea to have on hand for Tom and his friends. I had already made a lunch for them of potato salad, a veggie tray, and a choice of roast beef, or cheese and salami sandwiches, with chocolate chip cookies for munching. As an afterthought, I gathered a few apples and bananas and scattered them about on the table in case anyone wanted fruit.

With everything ready for a hungry group of men in a few hours, I settled by a window where I could watch the fence-building action without being in the way. I was surprised to see that without my noticing their arrival, the number of men had doubled.

As they began to measure the area, placing markers where the fence would go, I decided to email Collette. I wanted to send her some pictures of Brady that I had taken. I still hadn't heard from Rob so I couldn't write to him, but I made some notes about Daisy. I didn't want to forget some of the cute things that she had been doing. When I did know where to write to him, I'd have something to share with him about his dog.

When I looked up again, Wade was standing in the middle of things, hands on his hips, hair hanging in strings around his face, talking earnestly to Tom. My heart sank at the sight of him.

Wade looked annoyed, as he always did. Tom appeared serious but mildly amused. I debated ignoring the situation, but I knew I had to confront Wade about my porch furniture.

"Talking to him here would be better than going to his home," I decided. I took a deep breath and went outside.

Wade was still talking to Tom as I approached from behind him. The only words I heard were "damn nuisance," which I quickly decided to ignore. Tom had seen me coming, but waited until I was a step away before turning his body toward me, drawing Wade's attention to me. I returned Tom's smile of greeting and took a deep breath.

"Good morning, Wade," I spoke pleasantly in spite of the malice I was feeling in my heart. "What brings you out so early?"

"The noise! I could hear the racket all the way to my house . . . ."

"Noise?" I repeated, stunned. "What noise? I'm right here and I haven't heard any great amount of noise."

"Those dogs barked and howled all night," he growled. "And first thing this morning, there's all this rattling and clanking going on . . . ."

"And you could hear all this from a block away?"

"Dang straight!"

"Wade," I stood ramrod tall and stared at him as belligerently as he was staring at me. "My dogs, all three of them, were inside the house last night. They didn't make a peep. If you heard barking and howling, it was probably coyotes. As far as the banging and clanking, you objected to the height of my fence. It's going to take some noise to replace the fence."

"They're barking right now. Listen to them," his eyes blazed defiantly.

"This isn't last night. There's a lot of activity and people here now. They're supposed to bark when new things happen. None of this is hurting you, Wade. I don't understand your need to interfere."

It was his turn to look indignant.

"I'm not interfering! I wanted to know what was going on."

"So just ask. There's no need for us to quarrel."

"Quarrel?" he said, stunned, his voice incredulous. "I'm not quarreling with you. Lady, you are too dang sensitive. I don't know why I try to talk to you."

He pushed brusquely between Tom and me, his face a study in hurt feelings as he stomped across the grass toward the driveway.

I looked at Tom, who was diligently studying the activity at the fence, his face turned slightly away from me.

"Sometimes I'm not sure which one of us is crazy," I blurted out.

His eyes twinkling, Tom looked at me, a crooked grin playing on his lips.

"Well, I'm sure," he said. "And I wouldn't do much soul searching if I were you."

"I wanted to ask him about the chairs," I complained.

"I don't think he's the culprit," Tom offered. "I don't know how they're getting out there, but this guy's all talk."

7

Intruder

The next morning I almost ran to the front door. In my heart, I knew it was Wade moving the chairs. Would he dare to come back after our confrontation? Would the chairs be moved?

I opened the door with a flourish, eagerly scanning the porch. It was empty of furniture. The chairs and table were lying in the grass a few feet from the porch.

Confused, feeling shocked, I closed the door and leaned against it for a moment. He had come back in the night. What did that say about his anger toward me? Or was this his way of getting back at me for Moose stealing his bear bait during the night?

I felt Brady's long nose pushing into my hand, and I let my fingers close gently around his muzzle. His brown, almond eyes were studying me with a curious kind of patience. I often had the feeling in dealing with Brady that he thought I was a mite slow.

Looking up, I saw Moose standing in the living room doorway watching us, his soft, brown eyes alive with expectant hope. Daisy squeezed her head between his hind quarters and the doorway, straining to see what was going on.

"Ok," I said. "I'm coming."

When I started across the living room, all three of them began to churn restlessly, pushing against each other in their excitement. Yes, it was time for breakfast.

They circled around me all the way to the kitchen and stood transfixed next to me while I fixed their breakfast bowls. Three pairs of very serious eyes darted back and forth between my hands and their bowls. I knew the floor would be wet with drool by the time I had measured out their food and placed a biscuit in it.

"They were good dogs, all of them," I thought. "They don't challenge each other or attempt to take each other's food."

I had heard stories of dogs getting aggressive around food, and I was relieved that I didn't have to deal with that problem.

I didn't hear Tom and his friends arrive, but when I settled down in the sun room with my own breakfast, I saw the chairs were no longer in the yard. Someone had quietly replaced them on the porch.

I wondered if that someone had been Tom or if he had told one of the other men to put them back. The desire passed through my mind that I wanted it to be Tom.

My mind played with that feeling all morning as I prepared lunch for the men. What did it mean? I liked his take-charge manner, his sense of humor, his willingness to help me, and I loved the connection he had with dogs. It was clear that he loved them, and they loved him.

Was I attracted to him? Was I letting go of Chase? No, I didn't believe that. I would always love Chase. I wasn't ready for someone new in my life.

★　★　★

In the late afternoon, I heard the men calling robustly to each other in marked contrast to the mostly quiet conversations of the day. Curious, I went to the door and stepped outside.

Tom's crew, their jeans spattered with streaks of concrete, their shirts dusty from the day's work, were gathering up shovels and wheelbarrows and tossing them into truck beds. There were plastic sacks filled with trash lying next to the pickups. The work day was over for them, and they were preparing to leave a little earlier than they had the day before.

"We've finished the cementing and placing the posts," Tom said, coming up behind me, and I turned toward him, smiling.

He placed his hand on the banister of the porch and looked up at me. I felt a curious tug of feeling in my chest as I returned his gaze. His eyes flickered and he looked away, his brow tightened just a little. When he glanced back at me, I could see an unspoken question in his eyes.

It was my turn to feel uncomfortable. What had he read in my eyes? I wasn't sure. I wasn't sure what I had felt. My heart was so immersed in the past that the present was confusing.

"We should wait a couple of days for the cement to season well before we put the fencing up," he said slowly, watching me closely.

"Ok," I agreed, trying to sound casual. "Will you call before you come back, or just show up?"

"I'll give you a call," Tom said after a long moment, and motioned toward the driveway. "Looks like you have company coming."

It was Bea, her red hair flying in the currents of air rushing through the car. She tooted a few notes on her horn in greeting, as she waved her hand out the window at us.

A small group of wild turkeys, parading majestically across the yard, hustled out of her car's path with aggrieved dignity and annoyed backward glances. It was a grand entrance. Everyone stopped working and took the time to appreciate Bea's arrival.

She didn't disappoint anyone, trading banter with the men as she pranced past them. The mood in the yard had been busy but peaceful before her arrival. Now the atmosphere was charged with an energy that vibrated with excitement and a sensual energy.

"You've got some handsome men out here, Cathy," she announced loudly enough for all to hear, then giggled. "Why didn't you tell me? I'd have been out sooner."

Tom turned his face away, grinning. The men in the yard laughed and waved.

"Does Jim know you act like this when he's out of sight?" I gave Bea's arm a little shake.

"Oh, sure. He knows I'm all talk," she laughed. "And who is this?" She smiled up at Tom and held out her hand.

"Tom Ingalls," he said, taking her hand.

"I'm Bea Stimson," she glanced over at me with eyebrows raised. "Is this Dr. Barett's friend?"

"Yes and John Dunnom's. He's been good enough to bring some friends out to build a fence to keep the dogs in."

"How kind of you!" Bea exclaimed, taking Tom's arm. "Are you having dinner with us?"

She turned to me quickly.

"You don't mind my inviting myself to dinner, do you, Cathy?"

"No, of course not," I answered. "It wouldn't be the first time."

Bea giggled, and clinging to Tom's arm, tried to walk him up the steps, but he pulled back, a polite smile touching his lips.

"No, I can't stay. You ladies have things to talk about."

"Nothing that a man's opinion wouldn't help with," Bea held fast to his arm, and gave him an encouraging smile.

"Thanks, but . . . ," Tom demurred.

"Cathy?" Bea looked at me, with wide eyes. "Wouldn't you like Tom to join us for dinner?"

"Of course. Tom, please stay for dinner," I heard myself saying, parrot-like, and added more warmly. "I'm not sure what we're having, but we'd love to have you join us."

"See?" Bea smiled up at Tom and pulled again on his arm.

Tom looked helplessly at me, and I raised my eyebrows and shrugged.

"She can be very determined," I offered.

Tom smiled down at Bea, and inclined his head.

"Well, ok," he said, "but only if you ladies let me help."

"Fine," Bea said with authority, still clutching his arm. "You can do the dishes."

As she pushed him through the door into the house, Tom gave her an incredulous look.

"Dishes?" he questioned. "How did I get roped into washing dishes?"

Dinner was a riotous affair. Bea was in splendid form and kept the conversation lively. Her enthusiasm and humor were catching, and before long both Tom and I had caught her mood. We scoured my cupboards for something to eat, finally deciding to boil some spaghetti. In a moment of creative flair, we tossed the spaghetti with butter, garlic, chopped spinach, a splash of chardonnay and a liberal sprinkle of grated Parmesan cheese over the top.

We drank the rest of the chardonnay, starting with a glass while we were cooking, and a couple more during dinner. We did a lot of laughing, often times over nothing. By the time dinner was finished and we moved into the living room with yet another glass of wine, Tom felt like a friend I'd known forever.

As we relaxed in the living room, a sense of quietness seemed to come over all three of us. We were all exhausted, I realized suddenly. The meal, the wine, and the laughter had brought us to a place of quiet conversation.

I sensed, with regret, that the evening was moving slowly to an end. The problems I was facing had completely faded from my mind. I had enjoyed these few hours more than I had enjoyed anything in a couple of years.

"Did you hear something?" Bea said suddenly.

We all looked up, suddenly alert, listening. I began to shake my head when Tom raised his hand and pointed to the front door. Then I heard the gentle scraping sound, barely audible. The chairs . . . someone was moving the chairs. Had Wade been bold enough to come back with us right in the house?

I stood up, feeling anger flushing my face. Quietly we moved across the room and crowded around the front door. As we got ready to peek out between the window curtains on either side of the door, I turned the living room lights off so that we stood in the dark.

"Ready?" I whispered and got a hushed assent from Bea and Tom. I flicked on the front porch light, looking through the small window in the door.

A butterball of a black bear, totally ignoring the sudden light on the porch, was working diligently to move one of the chairs. I was too shocked to do anything but stare.

"That's a bear," Bea hissed, clinging to the curtain.

"I can see that," I hissed back, just as the bear's rear banged into the screen door, pushing the screen against the wooden door where I was standing.

Instinctively, I pounded. My fists hitting the door with an alternating rhythm that sounded like drum beats.

The bear tore off the porch, leaping past the chairs, and disappeared across the yard in wild fright.

I leaned against the door, my forehead against my forearm, relieved and scared at the same time, and felt Tom's strong arm slide across my shoulders. I moved closer to him and felt his arm pull me even closer. I rested against him, trying to catch my breath.

"I guess it wasn't Wade," I finally managed to say and heard him chuckle.

"No, it wasn't Wade,"

"It was a bear! You're not safe out here, Cathy!" Bea flashed, reaching to turn the light on. "That bear's butt slammed into the screen door. It was just a couple inches away from us."

"Well, it's run off now."

"Well, nothing! You're going to wake up some night with a bear in your hallway. Your front door opens inward. That bear could open your front door if he bangs into it hard enough."

"I'll put a chair under the knob until I can figure out what to do," I stated assertively.

I wished I hadn't drunk so much wine. My head was just fuzzy enough to be affected by Bea's fearful assertions.

"Where are the dogs?" Tom asked. "They didn't make a sound."

"They were asleep all around us, I thought," I said, turning to look about the living room.

They were there. Lined up behind us, all three dogs were watching us with interest.

"The bear was so quiet, maybe they didn't hear it," I commented thoughtfully.

"That's not much help," Tom rubbed his chin. "Bea's right about a bear being able to come through your door."

"I can't do anything about it tonight."

"Well, you have to do something," Bea yelled. "That's not a stray dog. You can't let a bear hang around until it turns into a pet."

"Nobody said anything about keeping a bear for a pet," I snapped back.

"I just can't do anything about it tonight. It's gone. The way he went off the porch he'll probably never come back."

"You don't know that."

Tom cleared his throat gently and we both looked at him, suddenly aware of how we sounded.

"It's late," I said after a minute. "We're all tired. Let's talk about this tomorrow. I do appreciate your concern, and I'll find a way to handle it."

"Do you want us to stay with you," Bea asked, but from the tone of her voice, I knew that she wanted to leave.

"No, Bea. I'm fine. I think the dogs would hear a bear that crashed through the front door. So would I for that matter."

"I'll be sure you get into your car," Tom offered, looking at Bea.

Then turning toward me, he spoke seriously.

"Cathy, are you sure you won't be nervous here? Do you want to go somewhere else for the night?"

"I'm really fine, Tom," I answered. "I've lived here by myself with Moose for over two years and with Chase for months before that. I've walked in the woods alone except for Moose. I've always felt safe. Anyway, we scared the bear off. I'll be OK."

He gave my shoulder a squeeze and nodded.

"You have my number if you need me," he said quietly.

I watched as they walked, barely visible in the darkness, to Bea's car. Tom stayed with her while she got in and started the motor. As she backed out of the driveway, he walked to his pickup, got in, and followed her out. He saw me watching from the window and waved at me through the truck window. I waved back and let the curtain drop closed.

I was alone. I was tired. I was also just a little uneasy. I closed every door between the living room and my bedroom that night, and kept the dogs with me.

"No doggy door tonight," I told them.

I assumed I would sleep like a log after the wine I'd drunk. Although I fell asleep quickly, I woke just as quickly a couple of times during the night. Falling back to sleep proved to be difficult. It had been a long time since I'd been held by a man. That little act of comfort from Tom had stirred a longing in my heart.

"It's the wine," I told myself over and over. "It's still in your system. You're not thinking clearly."

Lying silently in the dark room, my eyes closed, pictures of the evening began to dance across my mind. Tom's protectiveness toward me and toward Bea when he took her to her car, surfaced quickly. I liked his caring ways. There was a lot about Tom that I liked.

"Just because you like him shouldn't keep you awake all night," I chided myself. "Now relax, turn your mind off, and go to sleep."

And eventually I did. But my mind became very busy with dreams, disturbing dreams, about bears, and other big, uncontrollable, hard to see monsters.

I saw myself standing by a window of my house, all at once aware of a huge monster of a bear right outside the glass. His gaping, wide-open mouth revealed gigantic white teeth shining in the moonlight. I could hear him growling. I tried to hide behind a curtain, only to see the bear turn unexpectedly into a black, painted, plywood cutout that someone had placed there to scare me.

My home changed suddenly into the forest where I found myself strolling peacefully in the woods. When I innocently ambled around a large, bushy shrub, I disturbed a massive, black bear that chased me, crashing through the trees and brush. Ignoring my terrified screams for help, Moose continued to romp happily in Bear Creek.

When I woke again, I grumpily got up and into a robe. I wasn't going to try to sleep any more. It was barely five o'clock and still dark outside. I was thirsty, and my head ached. I tried not to notice that I opened my bedroom door very cautiously, checking to see that the hallway door was closed before I left my room.

"This is silly," I said out loud. "The bear left. He was more scared than we were."

But I just had to look outside when I reached the living room.

"Looking will calm my mind," I told myself.

I moved quietly to the front door and peered out the little window. I couldn't see anything in the darkness, so I flipped on the porch light. The chairs and table were in the yard, silent proof that the bear was back.

I felt goose bumps rising on my arms and back. I slid over to the window curtains and moved them just enough to look out. The bear was curled up in a corner of the porch sleeping peacefully, a big bundle of soft black fur, his face buried beneath one huge leg.

I dropped the curtain and flicked the porch light off. I certainly didn't want to wake the bear while it was still dark. I checked the chair under the door knob to be sure it hadn't loosened, and tiptoed back toward the dining room.

Moose and Brady followed me, watching my every move with curiosity, but Daisy stopped to sniff under the front door. Her tail began to wave slowly. She knew. She could smell the bear. If she started barking . . . .

"Daisy," I hissed, "come here."

Daisy looked up at me for a second, and then returned to sniffing the door.

"Daisy, NOW!"

To my relief, she left the door with a few backward glances and joined us in the dining room. I closed the door and led the way into the kitchen where I gave each of them a small doggy biscuit and myself a drink of water.

Back in my bedroom, I crawled back into bed, and cuddled under the comforting covers.

"That's one persistent bear," I thought.

The only certain way to make it leave was to call the DNR. They'd trap it and take it deeper into the forest, but they'd also tell me that I needed to get rid of the bird feeders.

Inwardly, I groaned. I didn't want to get rid of the bird feeders. If that's what it would take to make the bear get off my porch, I'd have to do it, at least for a while. The birds and other little critters were a large part of the healing magic of the forest, part of the intense life burgeoning around me, often unseen but never unfelt.

8

Connection

Tom called while I was having breakfast. The bear was gone. The chairs were lying in the yard. The dogs were fed and encamped in the back yard. And I was sitting in my kitchen sifting through my mind for solutions.

"I thought I'd check and see how you were doing this morning," he said cheerfully.

"I'm pretty good, Tom," I answered dispiritedly, "but the bear did come back. I checked during the night, and he was curled up in a corner of the porch asleep."

"We need to talk, Cathy. I'd like to come out and see what I could do to help."

And so it was that Tom was sitting at my kitchen table for the third time in as many days.

When he first arrived, Tom quietly replaced the furniture on my porch. Seeing him standing in front of the house looking at the porch with critical eyes, I went to the door. He saw me and stepped up onto the porch.

"Cathy, your porch is enclosed on either end," he pointed out to me. "That bear may feel he's found a pretty good den. He's protected on three sides while he sleeps, and he's got an easy exit if he needs it. The porch is comfy, and there's bird seed for breakfast just a few feet away."

"All true," I nodded. "So what do you think I should do? I'm open to suggestions. All I can think of is to call the DNR, and I hate to do that."

"That would probably be a smart thing to do," he agreed quickly. "I'm just wondering if that would keep other bears from trying out your porch for a night or two, now and then."

"Probably not, but I don't know what else to do."

"How about screening the porch in?" He gestured across the porch as he talked. "It wouldn't be that expensive, and it wouldn't be hard to do. The roof and floor are wood. We can build a frame, attach the screen and cover the seams with a decorative wood. We can put a screen door in front of the steps. I'm pretty sure that could solve the problem."

"If we're worried he could come through my front door, couldn't he come through a screened-in porch?"

"Right now, it isn't likely that he understands there's a door there. If he banged it in by accident, he'd see another possible den inside, and he might be curious enough to come in. But to deliberately and aggressively tear out the porch screen to take a nap . . . ? I guess it's possible, but I'm having a hard time imagining it."

"That makes sense," I agreed. "Bears seem pretty timid around people and houses. I guess that's what makes this bear's sleeping on my porch so scary."

Later in the kitchen, as I poured coffee for us, Tom looked at me thoughtfully.

"Did the bear you saw on your porch look like the bear that smacked Moose a few weeks ago?"

"No," I shook my head. "That bear was so big! When he stood on his back legs to confront the dogs, he was so tall! He kept going up and up and up. He just leaned over the fence and dropped into the yard, never even bent the fence."

"How tall was he?" Tom asked quietly, stirring his coffee.

"I'd be afraid to guess. Maybe . . . I think he was about twice the height of the fence. Eight feet? You could ask John. He saw him too. And Rob. Although he probably won't even remember it happened by the time he gets back."

I shook my head in awe as I remembered the bear.

"The dogs looked like toys around him."

"***Moose*** looked like a toy?"

"Yes," I said empathetically. "Oh, yes."

I thought a moment, looking out the window at my back yard. I knew what Tom was thinking. A bear that size could do some real damage. Sitting down at the table, I picked up my coffee cup slowly.

"It was really scary," I shared, my eyes meeting his. "If I'd seen him again, I would have called DNR. Maybe they would catch him and move him somewhere else."

"Bears can be dangerous," he agreed, nodding his head.

"I understand female black bears roam over a home area of about twenty-five miles and males seventy-five miles or more. I talked with DNR about the bears when I discovered them out here. They told me that I'm in what they call a bear corridor through the forest. I figured that big bear was just passing through because I'd never seen him before and I haven't seen him since."

I paused, thinking of the torn up bird feeders.

"That doesn't mean he's not out there, and I just haven't seen him. I don't see every bear that goes by here."

"I'll feel more comfortable about you living out here by yourself when the back fence is up, and the porch is screened in," Tom shared.

"I guess I will too," I agreed. "Although I don't think I'll ever stop walking in my woods."

"I can do the front porch over the next couple of days, if that works for you," Tom continued, ignoring my last comment.

"OK," I said slowly. "Tom, I feel like I might be taking advantage of you. How can you spare this much time from your life to help me?"

He looked at me, his mouth tight, his eyes searching mine.

"I have a lot of time on my hands right now," he said dispassionately. "I'm not ready to work yet, and I don't have a family anymore. Keeping busy here will help me as much as it will you."

I waited for him to elaborate, but he didn't.

"You seem to be working pretty hard, Tom," I said finally. "May I ask what you mean by not being ready to work? Are you ill?"

"Not really," he hesitated a moment. "It's a lot to explain. I was in the wrong place at the wrong time in Iraq," he continued slowly, carefully, not looking at me. "Mixed it up with an IUD . . . lost a leg . . . got burned a bit . . . . I healed, but it was too much for my wife. Our divorce was final a few months ago."

"I'm sorry," I stammered. "I didn't know."

"It wasn't her," he hurried to explain. "I had a hard time adjusting to everything. I wasn't the easiest guy to be around for quite a while."

"Still . . . ," I countered, "you sound like you just needed some time."

"Maybe, maybe not," he stared at the table a long moment. "The docs told me I was creating a crisis with my wife I thought I could control . . . to distract myself from the crisis I couldn't control . . . if that makes any kind of sense."

"Sort of."

He smiled wryly.

"It took me a while to understand what I was doing. By the time I had it together, it was too late for us. She was through. And I don't blame her."

"That's such a shame," I hesitated a moment before speaking again. "Were you married long? Did you have children?"

"Three years. No kids," he stated tersely. "She had a son from a previous relationship. He lived with us."

"Are you seeing him?"

"No," he shook his head. "I miss him, but she thought a clean break was best for him."

"That's a lot of losses," I mused. "A wife, a child you've learned to love, a lifestyle, your leg . . . ."

We were both silent, lost in our individual memories.

"That sounds so painful," I said, holding back tears as I thought of Chase and my own loss. "Losing a leg . . . I didn't know. That had to have been so hard . . . I'm not sure I'd even be able to comprehend what that really meant at first."

"I couldn't," Tom spoke quietly. "When you look for your leg and it's not there, you understand mentally, but there's no way to be prepared . . . ," he hesitated for just a moment and then spoke slowly, "for what it means to your soul . . . to your physical life . . . what you have to give up . . . what you have to learn . . . to live anywhere near normally again."

I nodded sympathetically, watching him as he carefully picked out the words to express himself so that I would understand how he felt.

"You can learn to live without a leg, with pain, or with scars," he continued. "It's your insides that take the real beating. That's where the hard work is done."

"Learning to live with an awful loss," I could feel my throat tighten as I spoke. "I understand that. It takes forever."

Tom looked at me with empathy. "John told me about your husband. I'm sorry."

I nodded, feeling my lips screwing tightly together. I was not going to let myself cry.

"I miss Chase," I said finally, "so much. I'm trying to get a life back, and I don't seem to know how."

I looked up, directly into Tom's eyes. They were sensitive eyes, and they were looking back at me, waiting. It felt like we were able to see inside each other's souls. I took a deep, deep breath.

"I wasn't physically injured, like you were. And it's been so hard for me. I don't know how you've doing it. You seem so together."

"I'm trying," he said slowly. "In a way, I've been lucky to be injured. Soldiers who come back without a scratch can still be dealing with some real demons. Because they look OK, they may not get the support they need to get on with their lives."

"John told me that no one comes back the same person they were when they left."

"He's right," Tom said softly. "It's hard to admit that you're in pain, that you feel confused. It feels like such weakness. Like . . . you should have been mentally strong enough to cope with whatever you saw, whatever you did."

Instinctively, I reached out and squeezed his hand as it lay on the table beside his coffee cup. He responded with a firm grip on my fingers and a penetrating gaze. I smiled at him, a little unnerved.

"I'm glad we've talked," I said, unsure how to get out of the conversation which had become desperately heavy for me.

"I am too," he said, releasing my fingers. "Shall we get back to outwitting the bears?"

"Yes, let's," I said, laughing with him as the tension around us lifted.

9

Running Wild

Trabor's Lumber in Traverse City is more like a department store for builders. The parking lot is a good four acres in size, spread around the one story building. An entrance at either end of the building makes it easy to get to the department of your choice when you're in a hurry. The sides of the building are colorfully crowded with flowers, trees, shrubbery, various garden gazebos, and arbor gateways.

Tom had called me after he reached Trabor's Lumber. There were many kinds of screen doors available, he told me, and he felt uncomfortable selecting one for me.

"I know it's a distance up here," he bargained. "So I thought I'd try to bribe you by taking you to lunch."

"Lunch is good," I responded, "I'm on my way."

As I pulled into Trabor's parking lot, finding Tom looked like it could be a formidable task. At least a hundred cars and trucks were parked around the building. Tom had said he had parked at the southern end of the lot, so I pulled into the first lane and started cruising up and down the lanes of parked cars.

A few spaces down the fourth row closest to the entrance, I saw Tom and a store employee loading boards and rolls of screen into his truck. He waved at me with a smile, and I felt unexpectedly happy as I waved back.

It was good, I told myself, to be working on a project for the house with a friend, with a man, especially when we had so much in common.

We made short work of finding a screen door. The big question was the finish and decorative touches at the midsection of the door. We found a treated wood door that could be stained or painted to match the rest of the porch. The cross section displayed a hunting dog and pine trees. It was a natural for my home.

Tom took me to Stefano's Italian Restaurant for lunch. His favorite hangout, he said. Stefano's was high on my list of favorite restaurants too, and we both knew the menu by heart. The hostess seated us by a window with a red-checked, double-tiered curtain. Our table boasted a classic, Italian, round, Chianti bottle in a woven, fitted basket with a much-burned taper candle in the long neck. The red, fake-leather, overstuffed booths were "sink-in-and-relax" comfortable.

Tony, our waiter, had served both of us individually many times in the past. Surprised to see us together, he clapped his big hands together and whooped, and then he blurted out that he had often wanted to introduce us to each other.

"Why?" I asked, glancing at him and then at Tom, who was leaning forward and grinning broadly.

"Both of you buy the same pizza. No one else buys that combination. I told you," he turned to Tom, "about this woman that buys your pizza."

"You did," Tom agreed, "a couple of times."

"So why didn't you introduce us?" I asked, curious.

"You were never here at the same time. So frustrating," Tony mused, grinning. "Now you've found each other without my help. So, is it 'Your Special' today?"

"Good with me," Tom turned to me, "or did you have something else you wanted?"

"No, that's fine."

Our pizza, with pineapple, tomatoes, green pepper, broccoli and onions, was served by Tony with a flourish. He dove the pizza down onto our table from over his head while making a trumpet sound. Several other customers clapped and whooped.

Embarrassed, I couldn't stop laughing.

It was a light-hearted lunch. We didn't talk about anything meaningful the entire meal. Everything either of us said seemed funny. It was a welcome relief from the tension of the morning.

★   ★   ★

The fun was over when I drove into my yard. Brady was lying in the middle of the front yard, calmly watching the birds in the feeders across the drive. When he saw me pull into the drive, he jumped to his feet and pranced happily over to my car to welcome me.

Shocked, I jumped out of my car and wrapped my arms around his neck as Tom pulled his truck up next to my car.

"Brady was running loose," I called to him as he came around the back of my car toward us.

"Did he jump the fence?" Tom asked. "Where are Moose and Daisy?"

"I don't know. I don't know," I cried, running for the back yard with my hand holding Brady's fluffy white mane of fur in my hand. Brady bounced along beside me, thoroughly enjoying the excitement.

The gate was standing open. The yard was empty. The house was empty. Both Moose and Daisy were gone.

"Who would have opened the gate?" Tom asked. "It was closed when I left."

"I don't know," I wailed again. "Were any of your men coming out today?"

"No," Tom said with confidence. "They were taking a couple of days to catch up with their lives. They wouldn't have come out without calling me. But even if they had, they wouldn't have left the gate open."

"How am I going to find Daisy?" I asked, stricken. "What if something happens to her? Oh, Tom, what am I going to do?"

"You're not worried about Moose?"

"No, he takes off all the time. He knows these woods."

"Maybe she's with him."

"Oh, I hope so. If she gets lost in these woods, we'll never find her. What if she gets stuck in a mud pit or some quicksand? She'd never get out."

"Daisy is a smart dog. But if you want me to, I'll go look for her," Tom offered.

"You don't know these woods either. I don't want you getting lost too."

"I know them a bit. My dad brought me out this way hunting when I was a kid, but let's wait a while and see if they come back."

I nodded half-heartedly, my hands stroking Brady's silky head.

"OK," I said. "I'll take Brady in the house."

While Tom unloaded the truck, I took Brady into the back yard and tested the gate latch. It was not defective. I was torn between concern about Daisy being out in the woods and anger at whoever was in my back yard and left without closing the gate.

"Wade threatened to kill Moose if he ever saw him outside again," I told Tom when he came in the house. "Maybe I really need to check Wade's place and be sure Moose isn't down there."

"You think Wade really meant it? That he'd kill your dog? He was that angry with Moose? He has that little respect for you?" Tom asked seriously.

"I don't know, Tom. I have trouble understanding Wade. I've heard he uses drugs and gets drunk a lot. Maybe he wouldn't if he was sober, but . . . if he wasn't . . . who knows what he'd do."

Tom nodded thoughtfully. "I think I'll run down there. You wait here in case the dogs come back."

"Be careful," I said, nervously.

Tom grinned, chuckling to himself, and nodded as he went out the door. I knew he thought he could take care of himself, but I wondered if he really could with only one leg.

I went into the sun room, Brady trotting behind me, and sank into my favorite chair. If Daisy didn't come back, what would I ever tell Rob? Who could have left the gate open? If anyone had come, the dogs would have been at the fence barking. It was hard to imagine a stranger entering the back yard of a house with three big, barking dogs.

Not even the meter reader would go into the yard after Moose started growing. He always had me call Moose into the house.

When Tom comes back, I decided, I would run across the road to my neighbor in the opposite direction of Wade's home. Perhaps they had seen someone in my yard while I was away. They might even have noticed the dogs run off and know which direction they had gone or how long they had been gone.

Fostering these dogs was turning out to be a bigger problem than I had ever imagined. What would I possibly tell Rob if Daisy didn't find her way back? My heart ached with anxiety.

"Wade said he didn't see the dogs, and he hasn't been down this way," Tom shared when he returned. "I didn't hear a dog while I was there. He's got quite a large family, doesn't he?"

"Yes," I answered. "It's his second wife and her three kids. One of his own, by his first marriage, visits him every other week. I wish they'd keep him busy enough to stay home."

"Well, I didn't see all of them, then," Tom smiled. "The kids I did see said they hadn't seen any dogs today. Wade called them out. He was quite decent about it. This must be one of his good days."

"Must be," I said quietly, my spirit flagging.

Tom sat with me then, quietly supportive. We shared several minutes of silence, each of us lost in our own thoughts.

"What am I going to tell Rob?" I worried out loud.

"Give Daisy a chance to come back," Tom cautioned. "If worse comes to worst, you'll have to tell him the truth. He's a big boy, he'll handle it."

"Want some coffee?" I asked. "This sitting and waiting is awful."

"Sure, then I'd better get started on the porch," Tom stood up, stretched his tall frame a little, and followed me out to the kitchen.

I was taking cups out of the cupboard when we heard Brady whining. Thankfully, Daisy was sniffing around the bird feeders. Moose was lying on the front porch as if he'd been there for hours.

I opened the door, and both dogs trotted obediently into the house. They passed us without a glance, heading for their water bowl, none the worse for their adventure in the wilds of the forest.

"If they get out again, I'm pretty sure I wouldn't worry about them," Tom observed, sitting back down at the table.

I handed him a cup of coffee and removed the cover from a plate of cookies on the table.

"I'm feeling kind of silly. I guess I overreacted, but Daisy's not my dog," I sat down across from him and picked up my coffee cup. "I feel so responsible for her."

"She looks like she had a good time out there," he remarked with a grin.

When Tom left a few hours later, the dogs were sleeping soundly, the porch was taking shape, and I felt genuinely happy for the first time in months.

★ ★ ★

True to her word, Bea called that evening, even more concerned about the bear after talking with her husband.

"You really need to be concerned, too, Cathy," she admonished me before I could speak. "Jim agreed with me. He thinks that having that bear so familiar with your house isn't safe."

"I agree with you both, and so does Tom," I said patiently. "There was nothing I could do about that bear in the middle of the night. But Tom is working on screening in the porch. He was here most of the day."

"Really?" Bea's voice went up a decibel or two. She sounded very pleased. "I am really glad to hear that! I liked him on sight. That's why I pushed for dinner."

"Because **you** liked him?" I questioned, teasing a little. "You've already got a husband."

"No, not for me. For you!" she giggled. "He looks steady. He has a nice way about him. And he's really quite handsome. I wanted the two of you to really get acquainted and have some fun together. You could do a lot worse. I'm serious, Cathy."

"I like Tom," I answered slowly. "I'm just not ready for a relationship. I still miss Chase so much."

"And you will miss Chase until you find someone else."

"It isn't that simple, Bea."

"Maybe it is. Just maybe you've grieved long enough," Bea said sternly. "It's been well over a year now. Chase wouldn't want you to stop living. He loved you. He wanted you to be happy and secure. Why do you think he left you that farm?" she added gently.

"When I'm ready, I'll find someone to love," I said, just as carefully. "In the meantime, I'm going to enjoy my friends, make new ones when I can, take care of these dogs, and try to find a job."

After hanging up the phone, I just sat, thinking about our call as the room darkened with the fading sun. I thought of turning on a light, but I began to wonder if the bear would come back again tonight. I was sitting in the sunroom with a full view of the porch. It occurred to me that if he did come back, I could safely watch him from inside the house.

Getting up, I flipped the porch light on and went back to my comfortable chair. Even if he didn't come, I needed to think about all the events of the day.

I was thoroughly exhausted. The dogs getting loose had left me shaken. I still couldn't figure out how the gate had been opened. And I needed to think about the budding friendship that was developing with Tom.

Bea was right, of course. Chase wouldn't have wanted me to pine for him forever. I just didn't know how to stop caring about him and about what had happened to him. He had been such a special person. He was so much fun. His sense of humor was hilarious. I missed the way he thought about things, his take on the world, and his love of life. It angered me that I could never talk to him or share my thoughts with him, not ever again. I didn't know how to let go of the desire to be with him.

About ten o'clock, I saw the shadows move at the far side of the yard. The bear emerged slowly from the night dimness, barely discernible at first. He padded softly across the grass, staying close to a line of trees at the edge of the yard until he was close to the bird feeders. Standing on his hind legs, he tipped a feeder, letting the seeds slide into his mouth.

At first, he looked like a large dog, and I realized that on all fours, he was only a little taller than Moose and Brady. His body was round and thick appearing, giving him a roly-poly, soft appearance that belied the animal's dangerousness. He walked by lifting one large flat paw, flipping it upward before setting it down, heel first, the toes flopping down rag-like.

Leaving the bird feeders, he wandered toward the house, staying close to bushes, my car, and then the side of the house. He moved deliberately, his large head swinging slowly back and forth, aware of every movement, every leaf touched by a breeze, and every object around him.

I wondered what he was watching for: possible food? possible danger? I felt awed that such a formidable animal as a bear should be so self-protective. I thought of how the dogs dashed about, without a care at times, and yet they were very vulnerable, as was every other creature compared to a bear. But it was the bear that moved cautiously.

Perhaps the bear knew how dangerous he was capable of being and assumed there were others in the forest that could be at least as lethal as he was. I pondered for a moment if that thinking translated into human behavior as well.

The bear appeared abruptly at my porch, moving slowly, back and forth across the front of the house. It found Tom's stack of lumber and smelled it carefully, walked around the pile, and pushed it tentatively with one big paw.

Leaving the wood, he lumbered back to the porch. After looking around for a very long moment, ignoring the steps, he hefted himself onto the porch. His head swinging slowly to and fro, he restlessly looked around again.

He began sniffing the chairs, pushing them gently with his nose, butting them with his head, pushing the chairs with his paws, and shoving them with his body. One by one, he moved them quietly and efficiently to the edge of the porch. With a final shoulder push, he toppled them off the porch where they tumbled to a stop.

With the porch cleared, he crumbled into a black mound at the edge of the porch and surveyed the chairs and the yard, his head swinging heavily as he looked carefully around. The light on the porch did not seem to affect him at all.

After a few minutes, his restless body seemed to get larger and larger as he rose slowly to his feet. Sniffing the porch, he lumbered slowly to the far corner and settled down to rest. His lower body lay on its side with his back legs stretched out; his shoulders were turned forward so that his front legs were extended out in front of him, chest on the floor. After a few minutes, he dropped his head between his front legs, his chin resting on the porch floor. His eyes were open, still noticing every movement in the yard.

I was afraid to stir, aware that he probably would see any movement even though I was in the darkened house. It seemed an eternity before the bear finally cuddled into the corner of the porch and hid his eyes with his burly arm stretched across his face.

I moved stealthily out of the sunroom, flipped off the porch light, and woke the still sleeping dogs lying about the living room. As they began to stretch, I motioned them into the kitchen with me, closing the door after them. It amazed me that the three of them appeared to have slept through the bear's arrival and den-making efforts again.

As I prepared to retire, I noticed that none of the dogs chose to sleep on their own soft, sleeping pads in various areas of my bedroom. They stayed close together and stretched out for the night next to my bed. Daisy's back was well under the side of the bed. They were engaging in pack support, I realized, and wondered if this meant that they were afraid of the bear.

If they hadn't been sleeping when the bear arrived as I had thought, perhaps they had been staying very quiet to avoid a confrontation. They were safe in the house. They weren't going to start a ruckus they didn't need to have.

I pondered if the encounter with the bear in the back yard had been more traumatic for them than I had understood. They had been intrepid in their response to the bear's attack on Brady. I questioned why I had assumed they had not been afraid in confronting this huge beast. Why had I assumed the incident would not affect them in the future? Apparently, it had been a learning experience they were not forgetting.

10

Breakout

At dawn the next morning, Tom coasted into the driveway with barely a sound. He was in time to see a sleepy bear munching sunflower seeds while a bevy of colorful birds scolded from nearby tree branches.

"That was quite a sight," Tom relayed to me later. "Those birds were really upset with that bear."

Tom shared that he had arrived in the early morning to see if he could see the bear. He was relieved, he said, when the bear scampered off as soon as he drove up, which showed it was afraid of people.

"I was a little concerned," he admitted, "that this bear might be more aggressive, or so used to people that he might be a danger to you or your neighbors."

"So you're satisfied he's just a run-of-the-mill type bear," I asked jokingly, awkwardly trying to cover my awareness that his statement conveyed a desire to be protective.

"Yeah, just an everyday bear," Tom laughed and smiled back at me, but his eyes were serious. "Just don't take chances with them, Cathy. Any bear can be dangerous."

I nodded my head, my eyes touching his for just a moment.

"I believe you. Is there anything I can do to help you with this porch?"

"No, not right now," he said, sliding his hand slowly along the handle of his chain saw. "But if I do, I'll call you."

"Great," I agreed, "in the meantime, coffee is ready when you are."

★ ★ ★

In the late morning, I went outside to brush the dogs. Brady especially needed brushing daily. His coat was silky, thick, and matted easily. Moose and Daisy loved the attention of being brushed, even though their coats didn't really need it every day.

When they saw the brush in my hand, all three dogs bounded over to the porch. Daisy's energy had turned her into the dominant dog in the pack. She asserted her right to be first and stood still as a statue while I brushed her out.

Moose knew he was next. His size alone made brushing him a formidable task. He had acquired some burrs in the fur along his back legs. I cut them out with scissors and brushed him quickly, conserving my energy for Brady.

Brushing Brady was a time-consuming endeavor. The back of his legs and his undersides were especially vulnerable to mats. While I was brushing Brady, Tom took a needed rest from his work at the front porch and joined us.

It didn't surprise me that I felt happy when he came through the gate. I had been alone too much, I reminded myself. It was no wonder that having someone to talk with made me happy.

Moose and Daisy crowded around him, and he petted them as we talked.

"Are you planning on staying out here by yourself," Tom asked after a few minutes, "or are you thinking of moving back to town someday."

"I don't have a choice with the economy the way it is," I answered. "Places just aren't selling right now. But this feels like home to me. I love the peacefulness of the forest, the many kinds of life in it. It's just immense in so many ways. It puts my life and problems in balance somehow. And it's a good place for Moose. He's a bit big for town."

"You'd need a big yard for him, all right," Tom agreed.

"I can't farm this place without a lot of help. Besides, I wouldn't know where to start. I hope to teach in town if the schools ever hire again. So moving makes sense," I shared thoughtfully. "But I've also thought of opening a kennel out here. It would be a lot of work, and I have a lot to learn about dogs, but I think I could do it."

"That's not a bad idea," Tom mused. "You've certainly got the room out here. Dogs love you. How about cats? Would you board them too?"

"I'd like to. I'd have to fix an indoor kennel for them, and I don't know where that would be. It's a dangerous place for cats out here. I wouldn't want a coyote or hawk snatching one. Cats are really my favorite pets," I confided, glancing at him with a smile. "And here I am with a herd of dogs."

"You need them out here by yourself," Tom laughed.

"Well, truth is, I'm very fond of dogs too. Getting a kennel started would be quite a job, but it would bring in some money. I really don't see a position opening in education any time soon."

"I take it you've been looking for a while?" Tom questioned.

"I've been to every school district for two hundred miles in every direction, and I check internet listings from all the districts in Michigan almost daily. There's nothing."

"Is there a related field you could move into?"

"Lots of them but I haven't any experience, and there are so many people looking for work that I'm not even considered when I do see an opening. I could get work as a telemarketer or in sales, but I'm not that outgoing, and, truth is," I added, "I'm still kind of depressed. I just don't have the energy to sell anything."

"I can understand that," Tom nodded. "Are you starting to feel better?"

I looked at him over Brady's back, as I drew the brush slowly through his tail.

"I think so at times. Then sometimes I don't think I'll ever feel normal again."

"I've felt that way," Tom stood up so that he could look at me over Brady's back more easily. "It gets better. Just give it time. And don't isolate yourself."

I nodded, then patted Brady to let him know I was finished brushing him. He jumped down from the porch, shook himself hard, and ran off to join Moose and Daisy across the yard.

Ignoring the fur on the ground around me, I sat down on the edge of the porch and looked at Tom. He had a healthy, strong body in spite of the burn scars I could see. His face was chiseled, his eyes clear and direct. He seemed to like me. I thought of Bea's comments about Tom and my need for a relationship.

"My mind knows that's good advice," I said slowly. "I wish my heart believed it."

Tom sat down next to me, studying my face. "Is there any way I can help your heart believe what your mind knows?"

"You're doing so much already," I hesitated, feeling suddenly nervous. "Just be my friend, I guess."

"That's easy enough," Tom smiled.

We both sat quietly. I felt distinctly uncomfortable and looked away from him, wanting my mind to focus on something else. I felt Tom's body shift as he also looked across the yard.

We both saw the dogs at the same time. They were gathered at the gate as if to greet someone coming. Then Brady stood on his hind legs, his front feet on the gate and bounced the gate latch with his nose. It lifted and then clanked back into place.

"No," I yelled, jumping to my feet.

Brady bounced it again with his nose, a little harder, and the latch lifted higher, hanging in the air for a second before it fell back. It was just long enough. The gate swung open under Brady's weight. He dropped down from the gate, and Moose raced out, Daisy in hot pursuit.

Brady sauntered out of the yard and glanced at us over his shoulder, his eyes shining with the awareness that he had done something special. We reached the gate in time to see Moose and Daisy race across the street into the forest, their tails high, and their feet peddling fast.

Speechless, I turned to Tom, who was laughing so hard he was holding his ribs.

"I guess it wasn't Wade," he chuckled, coming up next to me.

"No, it wasn't Wade," I allowed dryly.

Tom nodded toward Brady who was still standing outside the gate watching us.

"That's a smart dog,"

"Too smart for my good," I snapped back. "And look at him. He's so happy! How can I punish him? He watched the gate being opened, and he figured out how he could open it. I don't want to punish that spark in him."

"So what are you going to do?" he asked, still amused.

"If I ever get them into the yard again," I quipped with feigned concern, "it's padlock time, I guess."

"Harden the target," he smiled. "Good idea."

Brady eluded capture with ease. He explored the front yard, examined the bird feeder poles, went into the edge of the woods, moseyed down the street a couple hundred feet and back again, always staying just out of my reach.

His long, slender legs seemed to have built-in springs that could turn, jump, and go from a standstill to a headlong gallop in a flash. He thoroughly enjoyed my chasing him.

His eyes shone with anticipation when I would get close to him. His head would lower and he would watch me, holding his breath, his eyes shining, his legs splayed out in front of him. When I was inches away from reaching him, he would bounce away with a toss of his head and a wave of his tail. He would race off to a new spot to explore and wait for me to catch up with him.

I finally gave up and headed back to the house, and he followed me into the yard.

"I guess he'll come in when he's ready," I told Tom.

"We should catch him," Tom stated. "He'll know he can get away with this if we don't."

"He already knows he can get away with it," I said. "He's playing games with me, and he loves it. I think he's won this one."

"OK," Tom shrugged. "I'd better get back to the porch, but I'm here if you want help with him."

Brady stood across the yard from us. He watched as I turned my back on him and walked toward the back yard. I glanced back as I went through the gate. He had sat down in the grass and was still watching me. I went in the house and turned on the computer.

Fifteen minutes later, I heard the doggy door slap and knew Brady had come into the house. He went to his water dish, and I could hear him lapping some water.

When he came into my study, I put my arms around him and gave him a hug around his chest, pressing his head beneath my chin with one hand. I couldn't be mad at him. For a dog that had been isolated for the first year of his life, he was showing a remarkable ability to learn. I was too impressed with the cleverness he had displayed. He was a dog that needed a job, and I didn't have one for him.

11

The Hunters

About four o'clock, I took Tom a cup of coffee and a plate of cookies just as the school bus went by. The kids were all yelling out the windows as they passed. I couldn't make out what they were saying, but they appeared to be shouting at me. Tom stopped his framing work and looked up.

"They're excited about something," he said, walking over to me. "Is this for me?"

"Yes, I thought you might need a break," I answered. "School lets out for the summer in a couple of days. They're probably just letting off some steam."

As Tom drank his coffee, we looked at the framing he had built on the porch.

"It looks sturdy," I commented.

"I think it'll hold up," he agreed.

Just then Moose and Daisy showed up in the driveway. They weren't alone. They were struggling to drag a full-grown, dead deer between them. Moose had his jaws locked around one front leg. Daisy had a death grip on an antler. My mouth dropped open. I was literally speechless.

"Now that," Tom stated flatly, "*will* get them shot."

"That has to be what the kids were shouting about," I said, holding my forehead with my hand.

"Oh, my gosh, a school bus full of kids. Tom, those kids will tell everyone in town."

The dogs wrestled the deer across the driveway and veered toward the forest, dragging their prize across the grass.

"They're going to hide it from me," I stated, incredulously. "They know I won't let them have it."

Tom looked at me seriously for a long moment. "We'd better be sure how it died. If they killed it, it's a problem. If it's road kill, we can explain it away."

"I really don't want to look. I'll wait here."

Tom nodded and strode across the yard toward the dogs. He reached them at the edge of the forest just as Wade stomped into the driveway.

"Did they kill that deer?" he yelled at Tom, ignoring me.

"That's what I'm checking now," Tom answered calmly.

"If they killed that deer, I'll have those dogs shot," Wade bellowed.

Tom didn't answer but bent over the deer, examining its body. Moose hovered next to him, his brown eyes wide, his forehead furrowed, obviously concerned. Daisy wasn't so polite. Barking and growling at the men, she was becoming more agitated by the minute.

Feeling responsible for Daisy and not wanting anyone to get bitten, I ran to join them. I didn't look at the deer any more than I had to, but grabbed Daisy's collar so that I could pull her next to Moose.

She resisted my efforts, choking rather than move. I dragged hard on her, pulling on her body as well as her neck. She finally moved, and her barking stopped, but she remained agitated, panting heavily, extremely alert, her legs stiff, and her body quivering.

"I don't see any bites on the throat, or the back of the neck," Tom pointed out. "There's a bloody dent in the top of the head, the dogs couldn't have done that. Its back legs look broken." He lifted the deer's leg and it dangled crookedly.

"Someone hit it and broke its back, probably," Wade mused. "Then tried to kill it with a tire iron," Wade's sizzle had dropped to a sputter.

"It's still warm," Tom observed. "Must have been hit this afternoon."

"Must have," Wade agreed amiably. He had knelt down across the deer from Tom and was looking closely at the carcass.

"Well, I'm satisfied the dogs didn't kill it, just found it and brought it home," Tom stood up, wiping his hands on a rag from his jeans pocket. "You agree?"

"Yeah," Wade nodded. "That's a nice little rack. You gonna keep the head?"

Tom looked at me, and I shook my head, wide eyed.

"No, we don't want the head."

"You sure?" Wade stared at me, his eyes half closed, not quite believing his possible luck. "It'd look good in your living room. It's quite a trophy."

"No," I said firmly. "You take it, Wade." I stopped suddenly and turned to Tom. "Unless you want it, Tom."

"No," Tom shook his head. "The only hunting I do anymore is with a camera."

Wade stood up, quivering with excitement.

"I'll get my chainsaw. Be back in a few minutes." And he was gone, running.

Tom and I had barely begun to discuss what to do with the deer carcass when Wade roared back into the drive in a mud-covered silver pickup minus the tailgate. A rusty dent in the right front fender stretched from the door to the bumper.

All business, he approached the deer, chainsaw in hand, barely acknowledging our presence. I wondered if Wade believed we might have changed our minds and would say so if he spoke to us.

He had the head cut off in seconds, leaving only a neat, bloody stump of neck just above the deer's body.

"You folks are good neighbors," Wade allowed, nodding to us as he passed, laboriously carrying the head by the coveted antlers.

He carefully heaved the bleeding head onto the pickup bed, tossed his saw next to it, and climbed into the cab. With a last grin in our direction, he backed out of the drive with his treasure and was gone.

"I think," Tom said, "that you've just bought his good will."

"For today, maybe." I shook my head in awe at the change in Wade's demeanor. "I can't imagine getting that excited about a dead animal's head."

"You're not a hunter."

"Wade didn't hunt that deer down either," I stated stonily. "But he'll put it up in his house and act as if he did."

We were both silent then, watching Moose and Daisy hungrily biting at the bloody neck meat.

"That blood is going to draw every wild animal for miles around," I complained.

"I think you're right," Tom said. "I'd keep the dogs inside tonight. They'll be upset if something tries to eat that deer. They could get hurt."

"They look pretty wild themselves right now," I said. "I think they'd bite me if I tried to take them in the house."

"They're too busy with the deer to go anywhere," Tom answered. "John is going to come out when he gets off duty and help me finish the porch tonight. We don't want the bear wrecking the frame. We'll bring the dogs in when we finish, and move the deer into the woods. If it does attract predators, at least they won't be on your front lawn."

Grateful, I reached out, touching his shoulder.

"Thanks, Tom. I'd like you and John to stay for dinner if you can."

He nodded, smiling, and walked with me to the house, leaving the dogs to feast uninterrupted. As we drew close to the porch, I saw that he had the screen rolled out for measuring. The door leaned against a nearby tree.

"It's looking nice," I said, and left him. I could feel his eyes on me as I went into the house and enjoyed the warm feeling that grew slowly within me.

When John arrived a short time later, Tom pointed out the two dogs calmly parked around the deer feasting. Talking together quietly, they watched the dogs for a short while, and then turned their attention to the porch.

The framing was already finished, and together they made short work attaching the screen. Hanging the door was the final touch for the night. When they were fitting the door knob and lock in place, I stepped out on the porch, Brady next to me.

"It does look nice," I told them. "You've done a terrific job."

"I think you'll be safer," John commented. "It was a smart move."

Tom just smiled and nodded, continuing to work on the lock.

"You'll both stay to dinner, won't you?" I asked.

"I can stay," Tom responded quickly.

John smiled and nodded in assent.

"But we'd better get the dogs in and move the deer into the woods first."

"That's fine." I agreed. "Whenever you're ready."

"Brady hasn't gotten involved in this?" John questioned. "He hasn't wanted a piece of that deer?"

"No, he's been watching from behind the fence. I've seen him looking out the sunroom window, but he hasn't done any barking or asking to get out."

"So he's curious," John said, "It's strange he doesn't want to hang out with the other dogs."

"Well," I admitted, "he's more of a people dog. Anyway, he's odd man out. Daisy has a big crush on Moose. She's with him all the time. She seems to be imitating everything he does."

"Moose is one lucky dog," John mused.

"I should be so lucky," Tom observed ruefully, "having a beautiful female hanging on my every move."

"Like either one of you would have a problem," I teased.

"I knew there was a reason why I liked you," John laughed, turning toward me with a wide smile.

Tom didn't speak, but I noticed he stopped moving, his face immobile, staring at me.

Feeling suddenly uncomfortable again, I smiled and turned quickly away from them.

"C'mon Brady," I said cheerfully.

"Dinner's ready when you are," I tossed over my shoulder as I walked back into the house with Brady following.

I was just finishing setting the table when Moose and Daisy walked through the doggy door. Brady met them excitedly, sniffing at their faces. He knew that they had been eating something really tasty.

Brady looked at me with curiosity as Moose and Daisy went to the water bowl and drank greedily. Not unexpectedly, they ignored their food bowls.

I patted Brady as I went to the sunroom. The deer was no longer in the yard. I couldn't see the men either. They had to be dragging the deer deep into the woods, I thought. They'd be along shortly.

On my way back to the kitchen, I passed all three dogs curled up in various areas of the living room, resting. I breathed a sigh of relief. They would never get out again, I vowed to myself. I had promised to take care of them, and I was going to do just that. Those dogs would be healthy and happy when their owners returned for them.

★   ★   ★

During dinner, John suggested that perhaps it would be a good idea if they stayed long enough to see how the bear handled having his den disappear. I agreed promptly. The bear getting upset had occurred to me while I was fixing dinner, but I had put it out of my mind quickly. I hadn't wanted to consider any more traumas. I'd had enough for a while.

We turned the house lights off and left the porch light on so that we could clearly see how the bear behaved. As we settled in the sunroom, Moose came in, studied us for a few seconds, and came over to me.

His huge paw grabbed my arm, his black nails digging into my flesh, as he pulled my arm toward himself, looking for attention and petting. I disengaged his arm with difficulty and told him to lie down beside me.

"Doesn't that hurt," Tom asked, watching him.

"A lot," I responded, "but he's always done it when he wants attention. I guess it's just his nature, but I am trying to teach him not to do it."

Brady and Daisy wandered into the room soon after, found comfortable places behind our chairs, and settled down to sleep.

We didn't have long to wait. Moose, whom I thought had fallen asleep next to my chair, lifted his head and looked up at me, suddenly alert. His ears flicked sideways and then forward, facing the windows.

"He hears something," John murmured.

"I don't see anything," I said, straining to see what might lie in the shadows outside.

I reached out to stroke Moose's back and felt the fur on his neck stiffening under my fingers.

Almost imperceptibly, I saw the shadows moving at the edge of the road.

"He's in the driveway," I whispered.

"I see him," Tom agreed. "He's coming this way."

We watched silently as the bear, now fully visible, ambled up the drive. When he reached the cars, he nosed around them, investigating them carefully, even putting one big paw on John's car trunk and, half-standing, looked into the windows. He dropped back on all four paws and roamed past the cars to the side of the house.

"Shush," I said softly to Moose as he looked at me, questioning. I put my finger to my lips and shook my head.

"I'm afraid he'll wake the others," I breathed.

"They're awake but not moving," Tom murmured.

"The bear's out of sight," John said quietly.

"Not for long," I whispered. "Bears are so quiet. He'll just suddenly show up right in front of us."

"You've watched him a few times," Tom noted.

"They're around here often," I nodded.

"There he is," John muttered, "at the edge of the porch."

I petted Moose hard, hoping to draw his attention away from the outdoors. He rested his chin on my arm and stared into my face, still questioning with his eyes. Neither Brady nor Daisy moved or made a sound, but, very alert, watched us with large, curious eyes.

The bear moved deliberately the length of the porch, smelling the wood and the screen, his large head swaying as he walked. As he reached the end of the porch he stopped, smelling the side of the house carefully. He turned, retraced his path along the front of the porch, smelling the steps and screen, his black nose and expressionless eyes shining in the porch light. He turned away from us and continued back to the other end of the porch, where he stood quietly, looking around.

It seemed like forever that the bear stood, statue like. Then he ambled slowly away from the porch, toward the bird feeders. We watched, transfixed, as he rose on his hind feet and pulled one of the enclosed feeders off its hook. The bear shook the feeder and dropped it. Picking it up, he shook it again, but couldn't seem to get much seed from it.

Restlessly he sat down, the feeder in his lap, and grappled with it, his big paws enveloping it completely. Unexpectedly, he rolled on his side and then his back, his paws struggling with the feeder. He held it against his belly and then rolled it up to his chest, his hind feet kicking in the air.

"He looks like a big, cuddly puppy with a stuffed toy," I whispered. "He's really sort of cute right now."

John snorted, trying to stifle a laugh.

"I don't want to pet him," Tom shook his head.

After several minutes of struggling, the bear sat up. He had clearly gotten the feeder open as he tipped it up over his face, his mouth gaping open, white teeth shining in the moonlight. He dropped the feeder in his lap and sat, chewing, looking at the house. He was in no hurry.

As we watched, he slowly moved his head, his nose pointing upward, and became more alert. His head turned toward the forest. He rolled to his feet and lumbered swiftly into the trees.

"He must have smelled the deer," Tom said.

★   ★   ★

Tom and his crew arrived about three hours before the sheriff showed up the next morning. When I saw the squad car pulling into the driveway, I assumed Wade would be along in minutes. I wasn't mistaken.

Jim Jeffers had gone to high school with Bea and me. We had dated a few times, mostly football games, which he loved and I didn't. Baseball in the summer might have kept us together longer, but I soon decided I'd had enough of hard benches, cold winds, and hot dogs.

I could honestly say, "Jim, it isn't you, it's me. I don't like football, and I don't want to go to any more games."

In the way of small towns, we stayed friends, occasionally studying together, knowing that we would probably know each other forever.

Now, watching Jim climbing out of his squad car, I breathed a sigh of relief. Jim would listen to what I had to say. He wouldn't prejudge the situation. He was barely half-way to the front door when Wade raced up the driveway, his long legs covering the ground like a race car.

"What's she done?" he blurted out, hovering next to Jim as they walked toward my porch.

"What's it to you?" Jim responded.

"I live near here," Wade huffed. "If there's someone around here doing stuff that brings the cops, I want to know about it."

"If it turns out to be any of your concern, you'll know about it," Jim answered. "Now go wait over there." He pointed toward the driveway.

Wade hesitated, and then moved a few feet away, his face a thundercloud.

"It looks like you're putting up a new fence," Jim remarked, as I walked up to him.

"I'm hoping it will keep Moose inside," I shared.

Jim turned so that his back was to Wade and spoke in a lowered voice.

"What's with this guy? Dangerous?"

"Not so far as I know," I said, shaking my head. "More a daily nuisance."

"I'm checking a report about Moose and another dog killing a deer."

"They brought a deer home. Tom looked at it. He thought it was hit by a car. Do you want to talk to him?"

Jim nodded and followed me around the house with Wade staying a few steps behind us. Tom looked up as we rounded the side of the house and stepped away from another man working on the fence.

It was clear as they shook hands that Tom and Jim already knew each other.

"Is this about the deer?" Tom asked forthrightly.

"It is," Jim stated. "We've heard from several people that two dogs killed a deer and were dragging it down your road. The description of one of the dogs certainly sounded like Moose."

"They didn't kill the deer," Tom explained. "The deer had his back legs broken and a cut down the center of his head. There were no bite marks on his throat or neck. It looked like a deer-car collision."

"Where's the deer now?" Jim asked.

"We put it in the woods, away from the house."

"I want to see it."

Tom nodded and walked toward the woods with Jim and me on either side of him. Wade, scowling contemptuously, continued to follow us.

When we reached the area where the dogs had dropped the carcass, Jim stopped and looked at the area for a few seconds. Tom pointed out the direction the dogs had brought the deer, and Jim nodded as if he already had a good idea of direction.

Tom led us into the forest along a path which had been newly-formed when they had dragged the bleeding deer through the brush, breaking down shrubs and crushing grasses.

It was clear when we reached the deer that it had been a midnight snack for many animals. One of its legs had been chewed off and was nowhere in sight. The belly had been ripped open and the abdominal cavity was essentially empty. Part of the chest was chewed down to the shoulder bones, and the thigh muscle of the back leg was clearly exposed and chewed.

"Where's the head," Jim asked, looking at what was left of the neck.

"I have the head," Wade interjected proudly.

"How'd you get the head?" Jim asked quietly, turning to Wade.

"She gave it to me. I didn't just take it," Wade answered belligerently, pointing toward me. "Her dogs brought it home, so she thought she owned it."

"I'd like to see the head," Jim stated.

"For my report," he added, when Wade began to protest. "I'll give you a ride to where you have the head."

"Now there's a knife in your back," Tom whispered to me as he took my arm to help me pick my way back through the tangled brush of the forest.

"I knew it was coming. I just didn't know from what direction," I responded with a weak attempt at humor.

Wade marched out ahead of us, loudly complaining about police arrogance, their constant intimidation of the public, and this interference with his rights to the deer head I had given him.

Jim strode ahead of him without responding. As they entered the squad car, Wade was still grousing, and Jim was still ignoring his barbs.

Jim rejoined us in minutes. His cruiser rolled up the driveway and jerked to a stop opposite the walkway to the porch. He walked briskly up to us at the fence.

"I need to move on," he said. "It's busy today, but I saw the head and took pictures. There's no reason to believe your dogs killed the deer. It's good you're putting up a better fence. With someone like him around, you do need to keep your dogs confined."

12

I Wuv You

When Chase and I had put up our fence, we had done it with metal stakes. Sharp, triangular-shaped outcroppings on the bottom could be stood on to drive the stakes into the ground. Then we attached standard metal fencing to each stake with metal wires. We placed a gate at either side of the house and connected it to the fence. It was fast, easy, and four feet high. It wobbled a bit, and the fencing stretched some between the stakes, but it did the job pretty well.

With the exception of the bear, it had defined the territory as off limits to wild animals. Moose had been pretty good about staying inside of it many days.

The fencing that Tom and his Army buddies were putting up was taunt, perfect, and six feet high. Iron posts were set in concrete and a fence stretcher had been used to pull the chain link fencing tight. Metal bars were slid through the top and bottom of the fencing to keep it straight. The concrete went several inches into the ground and a few inches on either side of the fencing to discourage digging. It was an impressive sight.

A six-foot high fence gate on the right side of the house connected the fence to the house. A double gate on the left side of the house allowed a tractor or other vehicle to pass into the back yard. Another gate was put into the far side of the fence in the woods opposite the house.

"The gates open with this remote control," Tom said, dropping two small, black cases into my hand. "They also open with a keyed code of your choice."

"I didn't know the gate was going to work like that," I exclaimed, astonished.

"Neither did I," Tom laughed, "but after getting acquainted with Brady, I decided we'd better get creative."

"Well, thanks. I don't want to chase any more dogs than I have to," I told him, glancing down at the ever-curious collie nuzzling my fingers to smell the boxes. "The fence . . . it's just . . . I didn't realize how great it would look."

"You're pleased with it," Tom smiled. "That's what we wanted."

"Oh, yes, I'm pleased. I'm overwhelmed."

"We'll get the old fence out tomorrow," Tom promised, "and finish the dog runs. The guys need to get home now."

"They must be exhausted," I said. "Please tell them how grateful I am."

"I will," he promised.

"Tom, what do you think of a party for them? After they finish tomorrow or maybe Saturday afternoon, with their families? We could grill hot dogs, hamburgers, whatever."

"Sounds good to me," Tom nodded. "I'd think Saturday would be best. It gives us a couple extra days to finish up."

"I'll set up the croquet set," I chattered happily, "and a horseshoe pit for the guys."

"Do you have folding tables?" Tom asked thoughtfully. "Or chairs? Or do you see people sitting on the ground? Some might want to do that anyway."

"Tables and chairs—? I have one long, folding table, big enough for the food," I shared, "a few folding chairs. I could use the kitchen chairs."

"I'll check with the guys," Tom offered. "They probably have some folding chairs they could bring along."

★　★　★

I woke early the next morning, finally feeling free to spend some quiet time at my desk checking mail and email. Tom and his friends would be coming to finish the runs and the fencing. All three of the dogs were healthy and safe. Everything was falling into place. I felt peaceful, even powerful, as if my life was on track for a change.

I paid the bills which needed paying, tossed the junk mail, and turned to the email. Scanning down the list, I saw an email from Collette which had come in two days earlier.

"You need to at least check your email oftener," I fumed to myself as I opened her letter.

Dear Cathy

There were a few soldiers from Michigan in the group that just arrived today. I learned that Pvt. Dave Seymour had been unable to find a home for his dog, a Spitz named Sparky. He took his dog to the shelter in Cadillac on the seventeenth. It near broke his heart. Sparky talks. If you say "I love you" to her, she'll say it back to you. He's had Sparky a long time. I told him about you and he wants to know if you could keep Sparky until he gets home. He'll pay for her food, etc., anything you want, just save his dog. Please let us know ASAP.

How is Brady doing? I miss him lots.

Collette

The seventeenth! It was now the twenty-second. If the shelter was busy they could put a dog down in five days, especially a surrendered dog. Sometimes they put them down the day they came in. I didn't have to think about it. I grabbed the phone book to look up the number, and called the Cadillac Shelter.

It was a recording. Open from noon to five. Leave a message if you need someone to call you back. I left my cell phone number and a request to hold Sparky as I was on my way to pick him up.

I practically flew out the door, leaving three very surprised and noisy dogs watching me through the fence. Cadillac was forty minutes away, and it was already close to nine o'clock. I knew what the staff would be doing between eight and noon. I'd talked with shelter employees enough over the years to know that mornings were clean up time from the night before. Animals to be euthanized that day were removed from their cages and destroyed. I prayed I'd be in time.

I wondered if I could even get into the place before noon. If the doors were locked, I'd beat on them until they opened them, I told myself. I also told myself that I should just sit tight until I heard from someone. It wasn't common sense to drive thirty-five miles each way when I didn't know if they still had the dog. I left anyway.

I hadn't been on the road long when I started wondering if Sparky was a male or female, if it was neutered, or how old it was. I didn't even know what a Spitz looked like, let alone what kind of temperament it might have. What if Sparky didn't get along with Moose?

I'd never taken in a dog that hadn't been brought to my home by its owner. We had worked at getting the dogs comfortable with each other before the owner left. I might be making a huge mistake. But a soldier's dog? Especially one that could say "I love you?" I had to try.

★　★　★

Surrounded by the Manistee-Huron Forests, Cadillac is a growing town which has nestled itself around two inland lakes. Blessed with endless access to forests, small lakes, and rivers, the city has become a nationally recognized tourist attraction with forest trails, boating, and camping in the summer. Winter sports include ice fishing, one of the best ski runs in the state, ample cross country skiing, and snowmobile trails through the forest and countryside.

For all of its emphasis on the outdoors and sports, the community has a healthy observance of the arts. A lakeside pavilion and park showcases symphonies and other musical events, as well as craft and art shows. Festivals and regular decorating of the downtown area speak to a deeply involved community.

I located the county animal shelter in an industrial area of Cadillac where, I assumed, no one would complain about the barking. It was a long, low, red brick building with covered, chain-link fence runs on either side of the shelter. A green lawn around the building and a few flowering plants on either side of the front door spoke to a valiant effort to create a cheerful atmosphere.

Barking dogs raced back and forth in the runs as I drove up and parked. It appeared that there were several dogs in each run. My heart sank, knowing that multiple dogs in a run were a sure sign of a full shelter.

"She's still here," the shelter attendant greeted me when I opened the door at the shelter. "Be careful, it's wet in here."

She put her mop back in a bucket and stepped behind a counter near the door, wiping the palms of her hands on the side of her pants. Gray-black hair and dark eyes stared at me out of a face so weathered it was impossible to know how old she might have been. Her brown uniform under a black, plastic apron fit her wiry body loosely. Her name tag said, "Lil."

"I'll be careful," I said as I glanced around. The floor was certainly wet.

The office area had a small sitting area. Racks around the room carried pamphlets on caring for pets and state laws detailing the responsibilities of owners. A bulletin board at the beginning of a short hallway to a door, apparently into the kennel area, sported an endless array of papers and notices of lost pets, announcements, and state bulletins.

"We're kind of busy right now," Lil said tersely. "We've got to get the animals cleaned up, fed and ready for people to come visit them. Can you come back later?"

"Yes, of course," I said agreeably. "I wanted to be sure you knew that Sparky was wanted so you wouldn't put her down. I understand she's been here five days already."

"She should have been put down when she was surrendered. We've had a glut of pets being brought in. People can't afford them with things the way they are now. Lots of folks are moving and can't take their pets with them. But we promised Dave we'd do our best to hang onto her as long as we could so she'd at least have a chance of finding a home."

"No one has been interested in her?" I asked, hoping to get a little information on her personality.

"No one has been interested in any of the dogs," she stated dourly.

"Oh," I said, a little startled. "That has to be depressing."

"It is," she said. "There's some really nice dogs back there."

"I'm glad you were able to keep Sparky," I commented.

"She's Dave's dog. He's a neighbor of one of the staff, and he's volunteered here a bit," Lil shared. "One of us would have taken Sparky for him, and I think that's what he was counting on when he enlisted, but we've all got more dogs and cats at home than we can handle. Besides they're expensive nowadays."

"I can believe that," I murmured, thinking of my latest vet bill for Moose.

"What's Sparky like?"

"She's an older dog, around ten years, I'd say. She's a spayed, dominant female, so she's assertive. She needs a firm hand. Do you have other dogs?"

"Yes, three," I answered, my heart dropping.

"Well, then you know about dogs," she waved a hand at me and smiled. "Let me just go get her for you. The paperwork won't take that long."

"If she knew how those dogs run me around, she'd know I don't know anything about dogs," I thought wryly, watching her disappear through the door into the kennel area.

The door from the kennel area opened slowly, and a large white and gray Husky stepped carefully into the room, Lil holding her leash. One blue eye and one brown eye surveyed me with a mesmerizing stare.

"Is that the right dog?" I asked, startled. "I was told Sparky was a Spitz."

"They get called a lotta things," she stated flatly. "Spitz, Eskimo dog, Alaskan Husky, pretty much all the same. But, technically, she's a Siberian Husky. You want her?"

"Yes," I stammered, "this is Dave's dog, right? I just want to be sure."

"It's his dog. Call her. You know her name."

I pulled myself tall and folded my arms to protect my fingers, the way Tom had taught me. This dog was a bit unsettling. She was still waiting, staring at me. I felt a little like prey.

"Sparky," I said quietly, then louder, trying for a decisive tone, "Sparky, come here."

Sparky tipped her head and continued to study me for a moment. I wasn't fooling her. She knew she didn't know me. But, taking her time, she walked over anyway and smelled me daintily.

In spite of having thick, medium-length fur, she had a neat, well-groomed appearance with a sculptured look about her head and ears.

"If she was a person," I remarked reflectively, "I'd say she'd just spent three hours in a beauty salon."

The attendant thrust the leash in my hand, a cautious look on her face.

"Why don't you take her for a walk? Be sure you can handle her. She may not be the dog you want."

I took the leash and turned toward the door. Lil knew I was nervous around this dog, unsure of myself. I wished I hadn't been so quick to decide I would take her. I should have learned more about this dog, this breed.

The walk was non-eventful. She seemed to be more relaxed out of the shelter. I found myself noticing that her behaviors were delicate, even feminine. Her gracefulness showed in the way she tipped her head, the cautious way she sniffed the grass and bushes, the precise way she stepped, avoiding stones and messes on the sidewalk.

She minded well, changing direction easily when I turned, stopping at curbs when I did, and waiting until I walked again. She seemed very aware of my behaviors even though she didn't seem to be watching me.

When we returned to the shelter, Lil was not in evidence. I sat in a hard, straight, sunflower yellow, plastic chair near the door and waited. Sparky lay by my feet, the model of a well-behaved dog. I had the distinct feeling that I hadn't met the real Sparky.

"Sparky," I said, and she looked up at me. "Sparky, can you talk like they say?"

I leaned forward, and she sat up, looking earnestly at my face.

"Sparky," I touched her shoulder gently with my hand, and she glanced at my hand, then back at my face, her strangely colored eyes taking my measure, waiting.

"Sparky," I cooed, "I love you."

An eager expression passed through her eyes, and she wiggled her hips. Her tail flicked, and her front feet pranced slightly.

"I love you, Sparky. I love you."

Sparky put her head up so that her throat stretched upward. Her muzzle came close to my face, her lips and teeth parted slightly, and a half howl came out of her throat. The low howl continued with inflections up and down.

"I love you," I said again.

"I wuv you," Sparky howled, her eyes half closed.

"Good girl!" I clapped my hands, delighted, and hugged at her shoulders.

Sparky instantly became a different dog. She was no longer reticent or calculating. She pranced and danced around me, huffing and making little howling sounds. She bent her head and pushed on my knee, and I slid my arm over her shoulder and gave her a hug.

She hopped up on the chair next to me and leaned against my shoulder, licking at the side of my face. Obviously, those words were important to her.

"I love you, Sparky, I love you, I love you." I cooed at her, my arm around her body.

Almost shivering, she stretched her neck out and warbled that low howl again. "I wuv you, wuv you."

"You are a sweet lady, aren't you?" I patted her side, and she snuggled toward me, her eyes alive. The calculating expression had disappeared.

"Well, it seems like you've gotten acquainted," Lil said flatly, stepping into the room. Her apron was gone, and she was even thinner looking without it.

She went behind the counter and shuffled some papers. Finding what she wanted, she laid a paper on the counter, pushed a pen toward it, and motioned me to fill it out.

Sparky walked with me to the counter, but there was an eagerness about her step that hadn't been there before. Those words had been a connection for her to Dave, someone she loved and trusted. I had said the words she needed to hear to believe she would see him again.

She walked to the car, jumping in easily and expectantly, and rode home in the back seat without a sound.

13

Conflict

Two pickup trucks, including Tom's, a station wagon, and two jeeps were parked in my driveway and around my yard when I reached home. I wiggled my car through them to get as close to the house as I could without blocking anyone.

I could hear men talking in the back yard and sat for a moment, wondering what the best way to introduce Sparky to the other dogs would be. She was up, standing on the seat, looking over my shoulder out the windshield, occasionally glancing out the side windows. I could feel her excitement and curiosity.

"Well, Sparky," I said, "this is your new home for a while."

She woofed quietly followed by a low whine. Her eyes were darting around, trying to see everything, to understand her surroundings. If she had lived in Cadillac for any length of time with a young guy, I knew she had been in a forest before. But the male voices . . . she was listening for Dave's voice, I realized.

I slammed the car door shut and almost instantly heard Moose bellow a greeting, followed by Daisy's powerful barking, and then Brady's excited bleating began.

Sparky froze, looking intently in the direction of the back yard.

Tom found us before we found him. He brushed my dogs aside and started to hold the gate open for me, but when he saw Sparky, he quickly came through the gate and closed it.

"That's a lot of dog," he commented with amusement.

"She belongs to a Pvt. Dave Seymour from Cadillac. He took her to the shelter before leaving for Iraq. Collette sent me an email asking me to take her in."

"He'll be gone for a year, at least. Did you want another dog for that long?"

"Well," I hesitated for just a second. "Tom, I guess I just figured I could always make room for another little heart out here."

"That sounds like you," he smiled. "Is she spayed?"

"Yes."

"She has a dominant nature," he shared, watching her closely.

"You can tell that just by looking at her?"

"Watch her energy level, Cathy. The way she's looking at the other dogs. The way she carries herself," he pointed out. "She's asserting herself already. She's going to want to be the alpha dog in the pack."

"You don't think this is going to work out?"

"I didn't say that," Tom said quickly. "But I'd let them get used to each other slowly."

"Sounds like a plan," I agreed. "Is there a run finished?"

"There is. It's not connected to the inside of the barn yet, but the weather is good. She'll be OK."

I handed him the leash without regret.

"Her name is Sparky," I told him.

Hoping to quiet Moose, Brady and Daisy a little, I hurried through the gate. They had been lined up at the fence watching us with tails high and waving slowly, eyes serious, muscles tense. Moose and Brady ran to me immediately, almost knocking me down with their need for attention.

Daisy didn't budge from her position at the fence. She didn't even glance at me. She just stared at Sparky. For the first time since I had met her, her tail wasn't wagging.

Tom waited until Moose and Brady had calmed down and Sparky had sat down next to him before he opened the gate. Sparky walked into the yard and faced the other dogs with her head up, her tail curled strongly over her back.

Moose and Brady hurried to her, and the three of them began their doggy ritual of sniffing and touching each other. There didn't seem to be any kind of tension between them.

But Daisy was acting strangely, I thought. I watched as she stayed on the sidelines while Moose and Brady were getting acquainted with Sparky. Daisy sidled around the group, tail down. She slipped up behind Sparky, took a tentative sniff of her and backed away.

Sparky whirled immediately and faced Daisy, her front legs braced, the hair on the back of her neck bristling.

Daisy stood her ground, legs stiff, tail up, staring back at Sparky for a long minute. Then she started to bark loudly, frantically.

Sparky's lips curled, and she lunged at Daisy, stopped only by Tom holding her leash.

Daisy dodged her assault and stopped a couple feet away. Her body quivering, she continued to bellow from deep in her chest, a note of anxiety screaming through her bark.

Moose hurried to a safe spot beside me, his brow furrowed in disbelief, his serious, brown eyes darting glances first at me, then Sparky, then Daisy, then Tom and back to Sparky.

But Brady sauntered quietly and calmly, tail at half mast, head low, between Sparky and Daisy and stood there, not looking at either of them.

"Sparky, come," Tom commanded, pulling Sparky toward a fenced run.

Sparky let herself be dragged away. With venom raging in her eyes, she stared over her shoulder at the barking Daisy.

Daisy stood as if transfixed. Only a foot away from Brady's side, she still looked alone, isolated, her legs trembling. She continued to bark even after Sparky was confined. She seemed unable to stop barking, or even to move from where she was.

I walked toward her, calling her name, but she seemed unable to hear me. When I reached her, I touched her gently on the shoulder. She whirled around to face me, her teeth bared.

"Daisy," I yelled, "Daisy!"

She stopped, and I looked closely at her. Her eyes had a depth to them that made them appear almost hollow. She seemed totally terrified. She came to me then and leaned against my legs, and I petted her gently.

Moose and Brady moved toward her, touching her with their noses and bodies. They smelled her and stood close to her, and she gradually calmed down.

I looked up at Tom who had walked over to us after caging Sparky.

"I've done something dumb, haven't I, Tom?"

"Oh, I don't know," he said gently. "You were trying to help the Private hang onto his dog. But I wouldn't plan on letting them loose together. I'd keep Sparky caged. They didn't like each other on sight, that's clear."

"No, they certainly didn't," I agreed. "I'd better let Collette know what's going on."

Sparky just looked at me when I put a bucket of water in her pen. She was lying by the side of the fence a few feet from the gate. Her eyes were no longer friendly, but quiet, calculating. She was sizing me up again, I realized, and I wondered if Sparky thought I had betrayed her.

As I sat down at my computer a little later in the afternoon, Sparky's dislike of Daisy, and Daisy's apparent fear, were uppermost in my mind. I needed to let Collette know I had Sparky, but also that I had serious concerns about her. It was a difficult letter to write.

Dear Collette:

Sparky is now in my backyard! She is a very special dog and has "talked" for me. It was a delightful moment, and I am very fond of her already. However, she dislikes another soldier's Shepherd-Lab who has been living here. Sparky tried to attack her when they got close. We stopped her before it became a fight, but it raises major concerns for me. Has she been dangerous with other dogs in the past? How long has Dave had her? At the moment I have confined Sparky to a run by herself.

Brady is fine. He gets along well with everyone and all the dogs. He is unbelievably smart and very curious about everything 'people.' I just love him.

Hope you can get back to me soon. Take care of yourself. I think of you, and pray for you and your fellow soldiers daily. Please give Dave my email address.

Cathy M.

Late that day, as the men were getting ready to leave, Tom suggested I go with them to the barn to see the finished kennels. So with Moose and Brady, we walked toward the barn. Daisy started out with us, but when she saw the direction we were going, she left us and went into the Jack Pines alone.

The runs had seemed adequate to me when I had seen them briefly earlier in the day. But now with time to look at the kennels closely, I observed how large they really were. A good eight feet wide by twelve feet long, the runs backed up to the side of the barn with doggie doors into pens in the barn.

Inside, wooden fence pens provided the dogs shelter when they wanted it. In Sparky's pen, there was a nest of fragrant straw for her to lie on.

"Tom, it's perfect," I exclaimed. "This will pass any inspection for a kennel, I'm sure."

"The guys outdid themselves," Tom said, his eyes shining with pride. "They were invested in this project, not just for the dogs, but for Chase and you. We all knew him. A little of each of us died with him."

I didn't try to hide the tears that flowed freely down my face. For a long moment I couldn't speak. Words just wouldn't form in my mind past the feelings that raged in my heart.

I felt Tom's arms around my shoulders, pulling me against his chest. My arms circled his waist, my hands hanging onto his shirt, as I took a deep breath, willing the tears to stop. Brady circled us, huffing and whining with anxiety. Moose stood next to me, his huge paw raking my side nervously.

"Is she alright?" a gruff voice behind me asked.

"Yeah, she's fine," Tom answered.

Pulling away from him, I wiped my eyes and face with my hands and took a deep breath. Patting the dogs on the head for reassurance, I turned toward the men gathering around us.

"This is so great," I choked. "I can't thank you enough. I know you asked me what I wanted, but I had no idea it would be like this. You've really gone above and beyond what I expected."

There were smiles and murmurs of "Gee, thanks," "Glad to help," "Thank you," and other comments I didn't quite catch.

"Chase would be so proud," I told them, "of all of you and the kennel you've built here."

As they left the barn a little later, I reached out to shake each man's hand, and was delighted when a couple of them told me to "invite the redhead to the picnic." Bea would be all giggles that they had remembered her.

As the last man left the yard, Tom closed the gate and turned to me.

"I thought I'd help you bring some feed out to keep in the barn for Sparky," he said slowly, "and then invite you to dinner if you'd like to go."

"I'm kind of grubby, Tom," I answered, just as slowly, "and I really am exhausted. I think I need to get cleaned up and go to bed. Could we go to dinner some other time?"

"Sure," he responded quickly, "another time, then."

We walked together to the house, a light breeze cooling the late afternoon warmth, a comfortable silence between us. In the pantry, I found a large, covered, metal can we could use for Sparky's food. Picking up the big bag of dog food, Tom opened the corner and poured kibble into the container. As he secured the lid, he spoke suddenly.

"You're still in love with Chase, aren't you, Cathy?"

"I miss him terribly," I responded, being careful not to look up at him. "I miss talking to him, touching him. I miss his sense of humor. Yes, I still love him. How do you stop loving someone so important to you?"

"I don't know," he lifted the can to his shoulder and moved toward the door. "But a person has to go on living."

"I'm trying."

"I'll see you Saturday," he said flatly. "Call me if you need me."

And he was gone, his long legs covering the ground to the barn in what seemed like only a few strides. I waited at the kitchen door, watching as he opened the barn door and went inside. Sparky immediately dashed through the doggy door into the barn to be with him.

Moments later, he came out and closed the barn door, dropped the wood beam into its locking position, and strode to the gate. We waved cheerfully at each other, and he was gone. I felt a foreboding sense of uneasiness as I saw his truck leave the drive. I had become used to his presence. I liked him, but after Saturday he would have no reason to come back.

14

Ghosts From The Past

I haunted my email that evening and the next morning, waiting for a response from Collette. Daisy's fears were uppermost in my mind as I cared for the dogs and did my chores around the house and yard. Somewhere in the back of my mind, the thought began to form that these dogs might have known each other in the past.

I had been assuming that because Sparky had a dominant nature, she recognized Daisy as her competition for pack leader. But the more the issue twisted in my mind as I worked, the more I doubted my first impression.

Daisy had virtually abandoned the outdoors, I noted. She had spent her morning sleeping in the sunroom, even though Moose and Brady had spent much of their day in the Jack Pines and visiting Sparky.

Since I couldn't reach Rob, I called John midmorning and told him the story. I didn't know how long or how well he knew Rob or Daisy, but the possibility was there that he could shed some light on the situation.

"Rob's mom has had Daisy for years," John related. "I'm not sure where they got her. I never heard of her having any run-ins with other dogs. The only problem I ever heard about with Daisy was the loud, incessant barking."

"She hardly ever barks here," I shared. "When she does, it's enough to break your eardrums, but she usually stops when I tell her to. Until Sparky arrived, that is. That afternoon she was wild. She even turned on me for a second when I tried to quiet her down."

"She bit you?" John questioned.

"No. No, she didn't bite, just snarled at me. She stopped when she recognized me. She seemed to be in such an anxiety state that she couldn't see."

"I'll try to reach Rob's sister," John said thoughtfully. "She might know something. I don't think that Rob's mother is able to talk, and I believe Daisy joined the family as her dog."

★   ★   ★

Late in the morning, I started making a list of what I would need for the picnic Saturday. I found myself wanting to call Tom a dozen times to discuss the decisions I was making. But I kept telling myself not to bother him. He'd been at my house constantly for a couple of weeks. It was his first day away from my problems.

I was startled to feel a twinge of jealousy when I wondered if he would bring a girlfriend to the picnic.

"This doesn't make a lot of sense," I told myself sternly. "You don't want Tom to have a girlfriend, but you're in love with Chase."

"Maybe," my mind snapped back at me, "there's a difference between being 'in love' with Chase and loving Chase. Maybe you've come to terms with knowing he's not coming back, and you're ready for someone new in your life."

"I will always love Chase," I rebuked myself.

"No one says you shouldn't love Chase," my mind argued back. "You can still love him and fall 'in love' with someone else. It's pretty hard to be 'in love' with a dead man."

I threw my pen down and blew out a deep breath. I couldn't stand to think anymore. I jumped to my feet and headed out the kitchen door.

My sudden movement startled Daisy, and she followed me, her bright eyes curious. Moose and Brady were stretched out peacefully in the back yard, snoozing in the warm, noon sun.

"Ready for a run?" I called to them, running toward the gate.

Even with a head start, all three dogs beat me to the gate, which hardly surprised me.

The ground felt solid and comforting under my feet. Within seconds I had developed a rhythm, my feet pounding the pavement as I ran toward the two-track around my land.

Moose loped along in front of us, his long legs eating up the ground easily. Daisy's little feet were peddling fast, hot on his heels, her ears flying. Brady stayed closer to me, excitedly bouncing along on his spring-driven legs, watching me with his tongue hanging out of the side of his mouth, his eyes shining with enthusiasm.

Moose led the way onto the two-track where all the dogs slowed down, excited by the many smells suddenly available to them. I wondered if Moose had brought them to the two-track when they had escaped the yard a few days earlier.

I wished suddenly that I had thought to bring leashes, just in case they caught the scent of a rabbit and decided to chase it. I hadn't taken Brady or Daisy for a run without a leash before.

I decided to chance it. I didn't want to think. I didn't want to worry about anything. Clearly they had formed a pack and would stay together, and Moose would bring them home with me. I knew Moose thought of me as leader of the pack, and I knew he would not go far from me.

As they explored the brush, I passed them, still running, and for a few seconds wondered again if they would stay with me on the run or disappear into the brush. One by one they soon passed me, chasing each other exuberantly up and down the path, stopping to check smells, and occasionally glancing my way.

After a bit, Daisy dropped back, apparently fatigued, and walked quietly behind me. I, too, had become tired of running, and slowed to a fast walk.

Up ahead, I saw Brady and Moose dash past a rock lying a few feet from the side of the two-track. The rock looked strange to me, and I couldn't remember seeing it there before. But it had to have been there, I told myself. Rocks don't just get up and move by themselves. Still, I felt curious, and as I walked up the trail toward it, I glanced at it often.

Moose disappeared in the trees up ahead, and Daisy could no longer see her hero. Hurriedly, she increased her pace to a slow run and quickly outdistanced me, passing the rock without slowing down.

As I closed the distance between myself and the rock, I saw that it was really a baby fawn, folded up like a road map. Only its huge, soft eyes moved, staring at me as I stopped to look at it. Slightly more than a foot long, and about eight inches high, its long ears were folded flat against the sides of its head, covering its neck and part of its back. Its legs were folded neatly under its body and head. Tiny, light-colored spots were evident in the beige fur on its back. I looked past it, and about fifty feet away, barely visible among the trees and brush, its mother stood watching me.

Seeing the tiny fawn, I felt like I had been given a gift from nature. I took a last, delighted look at the fawn, and hurried on up the path, not wanting to disturb the mother or baby any more than I had.

I understood why the dogs hadn't noticed the fawn. When I was perhaps nine years old, I had gone for a walk in the forest with my father. We had found a tiny fawn that afternoon, and I wanted desperately to pet it.

My father had stopped me, explaining that the only protection a baby deer had was a lack of odor. From a few feet away, predators wouldn't notice the fawn because they couldn't smell it. If I had touched it, predators would smell my odor and could find the fawn. But even worse, he told me gently, if the fawn had my scent on it, the mother wouldn't recognize her baby and would abandon the fawn. It could not survive without her.

I found this information difficult to accept at the time, but learned later that many wild creatures, such as birds, respond to scents the same way. They will abandon, or kill, their offspring if it suddenly has an unusual scent attached to it.

Leaving the fawn, I settled back into a run until I caught up with Daisy who was hiking down the trail alone. She was obviously glad to see me. The larger, younger dogs had sprinted on ahead faster than she was able to run. Daisy, I had noticed a few days earlier, had a significant problem with arthritis, especially in her hip area. I would need to get her over to see Dr. Barett for treatment in the next few days, I reminded myself.

When we reached Bear Creek, Moose and Brady were already splashing happily in the water, apparently fascinated by the fast-moving fish whipping past their legs. I dropped onto the creek bank to rest and watch them for a few minutes.

Thirsty, Daisy waded into the water for a drink and to see what the other dogs were finding so exciting. She joined me on the bank within minutes, stretching out full length next to me. With her eyes half-closed, one foot gently touching my leg, she settled into a much-needed rest.

I watched her labored breathing and wondered if she was going to be able to make it back to the house. She was game, but she was still an older dog. The picture of her dragging the deer into my yard flashed into my mind, and I relaxed. She had kept up with Moose. She could certainly make it the couple miles around thirty acres.

I closed my eyes and lay back on the grassy bank. My mind felt itself being lulled into a meditative state by the many sounds of the forest. Listening to the water rushing over the rocks, the birds insistent chirping in nearby trees, and the rustling of the tree branches as breezes passed through them, soothed my spirit. I could feel a whisper of air on my face and hair, the rough blades of grass beneath my legs, a few drops of water as Moose climbed up the bank and shook himself dry before settling down for a nap.

It was peaceful, healing, my favorite hide away. I don't know how long I lay there, letting the woods and the stream minister to my soul.

When I opened my eyes, all three dogs were exploring the bushes and trees in the area. I lingered a while, soaking in the fresh scent of the crushed grass under me, and then got to my feet, stretching lazily. The dogs were restless. It was time to go.

Absorbed by the many sounds of nature in the forest, we followed the two-track around to the farm slowly, the dogs staying close to me. Wild life other than birds stayed hidden as we passed. An occasional grasshopper made a startled jump out of our way. Even flying insects seemed scarce. As we left the shade of the woods, the sun felt warm and soothing, yet energizing.

If Tom ever does indicate a personal interest in me, I thought suddenly, I would want to share Bear Creek with him. It was a place he would like.

"Does that mean," I asked myself, "that you would welcome his interest in you? Are you ready?"

"I'm always ready for a friend," I told myself, evading the question even from myself.

But I called Tom when I got home. He wasn't home, so I left a message for him to call if he wanted to add anything to the picnic preparations I was planning.

As I opened my email, I wondered idly where he was, and what he might be doing. My musing was cut short as I saw an email from Collette.

Hi Cathy,

I talked with Dave and gave him your email address. He'll write soon. He said that when Sparky was a year old, his dad brought home a puppy they named Loco. He isn't sure of the breed. The two dogs never got along. Loco was a nervous puppy and barked constantly, which agitated Sparky. They did fight often, and Loco, being a puppy, always lost and was often hurt. Dave's father eventually gave Loco to a family looking for a dog. Dave didn't know them. That was years ago. He said Sparky loves people. He's never heard of her having a problem with any dog other than Loco.

I'm glad Brady is getting along well. Thanks for the pictures. He looks well and happy. I sent a check to you through my bank yesterday.

Collette

I emailed her back immediately.

Thanks for sending the check and the info, Collette. I'm keeping Sparky in a kennel. She's just too hostile to Daisy, and I don't want either dog getting hurt. I'll be sure she gets out for a run every day. Moose and Brady are spending a lot of time hanging around her run and keeping her company. I'm sure she'll be fine here. I haven't heard from Dave so please let him know.

Cathy M.

"Well," I thought, closing my computer, "that's the best I can do with that situation. I need to get back to planning the picnic.

There's food to buy and prepare. The croquet set to get out and set up. Horseshoes and a couple spikes to find in the barn and clean. I'd probably better pick up some balls for the kids, and maybe a badminton set."

As I thought of the work I had to finish in the next day-and-a-half, reality caught up with me. Not getting finished before people arrived Saturday was a very real possibility. I grabbed my grocery list and ran for the car.

Bea had offered to make a potato salad when I invited her and Jim. I had called the market and ordered a sheet cake with a fence and dog decorations on it. Bea would pick it up on her way out Saturday. Some of Tom's friends were bringing chairs.

The guys would want to set up the horseshoe pits. I could always set up the croquet court after people were there. I took a deep breath and told myself to calm down. Everything would get done.

I was just pulling into Barton's Grocery Outlet when Tom reached me on my cell phone.

"I'm glad you called," I said cheerfully. "I wanted to run things by you and be sure your friends will like the food I'm planning."

"As long as you're not serving frozen dinners, they'll love it," Tom joked.

"Nothing frozen but ice cream," I teased back. "The usual picnic stuff: baked beans, potato salad, chips, hot dogs and hamburgers. Or would it be better if we had fried chicken?"

"Fried chicken can be a lot of work," he countered. "We can grill hot dogs, brats, and burgers without a lot of fuss."

"I thought grilling ears of corn might be fun," I suggested.

"Where are you?" he asked suddenly. "I can hear a lot of traffic."

"I'm at Barton's."

"I'm not far from there. Why don't you get started with your shopping, and I'll meet you there in a few minutes."

As I walked into Barton's, I felt a definite sense of happiness. I had wanted him to meet me. More importantly, I had wanted him to want to meet me. I couldn't deny that he was important to me anymore. I liked sharing ideas and activities with him. He brought a restrained kind of excitement with him.

As I wheeled my basket through the aisles, I found myself wondering what he would be like if he felt I was interested in him.

I thought about him so much in the next few minutes that when he suddenly showed up next to me, I felt shy.

"Is something the matter?" he asked, looking at me quizzically.

"No, nothing," I stammered. "Why?"

"You look like you got caught with your hand in the cookie jar," smiling that crooked smile, his eyes squinted just a little as he looked at me.

"Oh," I kidded back, "more like my mind was in the cookie jar."

"Now that sounds promising," he said with an understated energy but his eyes twinkled. A tiny dimple I hadn't noticed before played at the corner of his lips.

"Food, just food," I said quickly, with a laugh. "Shopping always makes me think of endless possibilities for dinner."

"Dinner, huh?" he nodded his head slowly, placed his hand on the side of the shopping cart, and leaned a little toward me.

I could feel my face beginning to smile with a responsive excitement.

"Now if I asked you to dinner again, would you turn me down again?" he asked, pursing his lips just a little.

"Tom!" I exclaimed, feigning shock. "No, of course not. But there's so much to do. Do we have time?"

"You're already in town. You have to eat, I have to eat. Let's get this shopping done and have some fun."

"Fun," I repeated slowly, drawing the word out. "It's been a while. Let's do it."

Over dinner, I found myself studying Tom. He looked different to me than he had before. He had seemed a tall and rather slender man, but now I was aware that he was a larger man than I had been seeing. His hands were strong, capable, with long muscled fingers.

"No wonder he was able to pick up the lawn chairs so easily," I thought, thinking back to the first time we had met.

The dimple at the side of his mouth was small but very evident, yet I had never noticed it before today. How many times had I looked at Tom and never really seen him?

I began to wonder if the depression I'd been in had stopped me from seeing other people, other situations, clearly. Wade? Was he as ornery as I thought he was? I wasn't wrong there. Jim had wondered if he was dangerous, and Tom had clearly said my impressions of Wade were right on.

No, it was Tom I had been having trouble seeing clearly. Why just Tom? He had always been kind to me, even looking for ways to help me. He was so understanding of my situation. I wondered suddenly if that frightened me.

Was I afraid to be involved with a man again? Was I afraid of being hurt again? It was possible. Was I holding onto Chase because I loved him, or to protect myself? The thought made my insides cringe, and I shivered suddenly.

"Are you cold?" I heard Tom ask.

"No," I responded quickly. "I'm fine."

He looked at me critically for a moment, and then nodded.

"OK," he said. "I've been thinking I'd follow you home and help you get the groceries into the house."

"It's a long way, Tom." I demurred. "I only need to get the perishables into the house. I can bring the rest in tomorrow."

"I'd rather," Tom insisted. "It'll be dark, and I don't want you struggling with those boxes at the same time you're trying to out run a bear."

"Now, there's a picture," I laughed.

We sat quietly then in a companionable silence, finishing the last bites of our dinners.

"Tom, I'd like to ask you something," I said hesitantly.

"Sure, Cathy," he looked at me expectantly.

"Yesterday, I asked you if you knew how to stop loving someone, and you said you didn't."

"Yeah," he nodded, his forehead wrinkling in thought.

"Do you still love your ex-wife?"

"Brenda," He spoke slowly. "Her name is Brenda. I have feelings about her, but not like you seem to have for Chase. She's with another guy. She's out of my life."

"Oh."

"I don't think about her. I try to stay focused on today, on the future, on what I can have in my life."

"I'm doing better with that recently," I said slowly.

He nodded, and smiled.

"You're building quite a little ranch out there."

"I couldn't have done it without you and your friends."

"We were glad to help. But you'd have gotten it done on your own."

"I wonder about that," I answered slowly. "I didn't have a clue where to start."

"But you knew what you wanted done," he responded thoughtfully.

15

The Picnic

Saturday morning. I woke up feeling the pressure of all that still had to be done to get ready for the picnic. Tom had surprised me Friday afternoon, stopping by to help set things up.

He had hauled the long folding table I was planning to use for food from the basement, and set it up in the yard near the outside stairs. He carried my kitchen and folding chairs outside, setting them in little groups around the yard, and adding four chairs of his own that he had brought out.

"You'll need something to sit on for coffee," he had remarked, leaving one chair in the kitchen. I noted that he was again thinking of my comfort.

Tom seemed to take pleasure in setting up the grill, making sure the charcoal was handy and of a type that would burn easily. Afterwards, he joined me in setting up the croquet court near the Jack Pines.

In spite of our time crunch, we found ourselves engaging in a spontaneous attempt at croquet, which left both of us humbled and laughing hysterically.

Avoiding any attempt at a rematch, I headed into the kitchen to start the baking and Tom disappeared into the old barn. He found a number of used horseshoes and cleaned them, a dirty job if ever there was one.

We couldn't find large enough spikes for the pits. He measured out some ground near the barn and dug the pits for the spikes anyway, placing four horseshoes invitingly in each pit.

Before Tom left, he tied the badminton net up between the clothes line poles, and promised to stop at Trabor's Lumber to pick up a couple spikes on his way out Saturday.

Bea had called Friday evening to see if I needed her to pick up anything else. We talked more about Tom than the picnic. She was firmly convinced that he was a special guy.

"He's really looking out for you," she had said strongly. "You can't make a guy do that. He has to be attracted to you. You need to stop your grieving widow act and encourage him."

"It's not an act," I hissed at her. "And I am being nice to him."

"I mean really nice," she emphasized.

"I'll see you tomorrow," I said and hung up. Sometimes Bea really irritated me.

★   ★   ★

But I was glad to see her and Jim when they rolled into my driveway, loaded with potato salad and a huge sheet cake, boxed neatly in a plastic shell.

"That's enough potato salad for an army," I observed.

"Bea said you invited the Army," Jim laughed, giving me a hug.

I hugged him back, feeling his muscled roundness pressing against me. He was a gentle giant of a man. Well over six foot, he towered over Bea and me. His black hair was sleek and straight, his brown eyes set between finely crinkled lines at his temples. His nose was straight, his cheekbones prominent above firmly marked lips. His American Indian heritage was clearly evident.

His distinctiveness was a perfect foil for Bea's flamboyance. But his manner was what endeared him to me. Easy going and sensitive, he watched Bea slash her way through life with amusement, protectiveness and pride. They couldn't have been more different in personality, but their union was cast in iron.

The cake drew ooh's, aah's and laughs from everyone as they arrived. The cake decorator had shown her artistic talent with comic forcefulness. She had drawn four frosting dogs: a big black dog, a brown dog with a white chest, a brown dog with a black saddle, and a gray and white dog. All of the dogs evinced the most forlorn expressions, their eyes huge and sad.

They were standing behind a most intimidating barbed-wire fence, while a deer and two rabbits stared at them from the other side of the fence. Behind the dogs was green grass, but around the rabbits and deer, flowers of different colors graced the grass. On the fence facing the wild animals hung a "No Trespassing" sign.

The men began arriving with their wives, and it seemed that every couple brought several children along. It turned out that almost every child had wanted to bring a friend, and in many cases parents had agreed. I lost count at thirty children of all ages from infants to teens.

After about ten kids had arrived, Jim suggested putting Moose, Brady and Daisy in one of the open kennels.

"Just to be on the safe side," Jim said. "You never know how kids are going to act with animals or how the animals will react to the kids."

I agreed. I had often been surprised at how uninformed many adults, including myself, were about dogs and how to interact with them safely.

When Tom arrived and saw the dogs penned up, he supported our decision.

"It's a good idea," he said. "The dogs don't know these people. With all the noise and running around that's going on, the dogs will be excited. Dogs think they're being attacked when a person or another animal runs at them, so someone getting bitten would almost be inevitable—probably a kid."

"So we've dodged a bullet," I said with satisfaction. "That's a relief."

I was pleased, as the afternoon wore on, to see that people really did seem to be enjoying themselves. Everyone seemed to know at least some of the other people there and many of them knew everyone. They were happy to have the chance to see each other again. It wasn't long before every game was being played with laughter and excited shouting. In addition, a spontaneous baseball game had sprung up in the front yard.

The gentle thud of rackets hitting the badminton cock were drowned out by the clacking sounds of the croquet mallets hitting the wooden balls and the sharp ringing sounds of the horseshoes striking the spikes.

The cheers and competitive shouts from all four groups sailed through the air like a boisterous symphony. The occasional child's high pitched voice or the cries of an infant kept the sounds of excitement grounded in a pastoral reality.

All went well, at least for a while.

I was getting acquainted with Mavis, the wife of a retired Sergeant who had worked tirelessly on the fencing, when I heard a scream from the area of the barn.

"Who let the dogs out?" a man's voice yelled.

"Dog fight," yelled another male voice.

Mavis and I both whirled around in time to see Sparky, tail up, fur bristling, advancing on Daisy who was sidestepping away from the bigger dog. As Daisy backed up, she became pinned against the side of the kennel fence with Sparky advancing menacingly.

Brady appeared out of nowhere, and calmly, quietly, walked between the two of them, head and tail down, as he had that first afternoon. He just stood there, looking toward me, now racing across the yard toward them.

Daisy huddled against the fence, peering around Brady's legs toward me.

Sparky stood aggressively at Brady's side, cut off from Daisy, but still ready for a fight.

Moose raced up suddenly beside them, and Brady turned his head to look at him.

Brady's sudden movement released something in Sparky, and she tore at Brady, grabbing his shoulder with her teeth.

Brady yelped, twisting himself free as Moose grabbed Sparky by the back of the neck, knocking her away from Brady.

Moose, his legs bent at the knees, stared at Sparky, who whirled instantly around to face him. Sparky looked at Moose, easily more than twice her size, and, no coward, braced herself for a fight.

Moose lowered his head, his eyes intently staring at her, his shoulders wide. Sparky moved her feet restlessly, her lips curling, her eyes glittering.

I opened the door to Sparky's kennel and called her sharply. She backed up a couple of steps, then turned and ran toward me and the safety of her kennel. I closed the door on her, latched the lock and turned to Moose.

I wrapped my arms around his neck and gave him a hug. I could feel the energy pulsing inside of his muscles. He was still on guard.

"Come, Moose," I said softly, walking toward the far kennel, my arm draped loosely around his neck. Out of the corner of my eye, I could see that Tom, Jim and some other men were bent over Brady. Daisy was still huddled beside the fence. She seemed afraid to move.

I opened the kennel door and motioned Moose inside. Daisy hurried over to be with Moose, and I shut the kennel door behind her.

I knew Brady had been bitten. How badly I didn't know. Walking over to him seemed to take minutes, but it couldn't have taken more than a few seconds.

When Brady saw me coming, he pulled away from the men and walked into my arms, pushing his face into my shoulder. I held him for a long moment, my head over his, cuddling him into my body. He was still trembling. The wound on his shoulder was bleeding.

"It's a good-sized gash," Tom informed me, leaning over us. "The bite ripped through his hide."

"I'd better get him to Dr. Barett," I responded.

"I'll go with you," he said.

"Tom, we need to check Sparky," I shared, standing up. "I think Moose bit her. She could be hurt too."

"I'll hold Brady," Jim said, coming up next to us, and reaching for Brady.

"Jim, could you put Brady in my car, please?" I asked him, and he nodded.

As we entered her kennel, Sparky met us, acting peaceful and welcoming. She let us check her back and legs. She walked around the enclosure with us without a sign of discomfort or anger. There were no bite marks on her back.

"She has such thick fur," Tom noted. "I don't think Moose hurt her. He just let her know he could."

"I'm so proud of him," I murmured, "Brady, too. That's the second time Brady has gotten between Sparky and Daisy. I think he was trying to give Daisy some cover and Sparky time to calm down."

"They're both brave dogs," Tom agreed.

We left Sparky's kennel together, and faced the concerned crowd of people standing around the pens.

"Well," I said, "our picnic's had a little interruption. Brady has an open bite, and I need to take him to the vet right now, but that shouldn't stop our picnic. We'll be back shortly. The other dogs are fine, but they were in the kennels for a reason. Please don't let them out again."

"It was these boys that done it," a man's voice said. "They didn't come with us."

I looked at him, recognizing him as one of the men who had worked daily on the fence. A big man, he had a firm, tanned face under graying hair. Now his big hands were resting on the shoulders of two boys about fourteen years of age. Dressed in tee shirts and blue jeans, their faces were tense with emotion, but there was also a hardness in their eyes that I found disturbing.

"Who are you?" I asked. There was no answer from either of them.

"Who invited you here?" There was still no answer from them, just a sullen silence.

"I think I saw you at Wade's home last week," remarked Tom, standing close to me and looking at the younger of the two. "What's your name?"

The boy looked at the other boy for a second and then back to Tom. With a shrug, he finally spoke.

"Lee. We didn't mean no harm. We felt sorry for the dogs all cooped up. Everyone's having a good time but them."

"Do you understand now why they were in kennels?" I asked. "Yeah."

"Did someone invite you here?" I asked again.

"We saw all the cars coming and walked down. There were so many people here, we figured no one would notice us," he stopped and looked at the older boy who gave him a hard look, and then stared silently at me.

"You're not invisible, Lee, but you would have been welcome. Now, you do need to leave. Don't come here again without an invitation," I said sternly.

"You gonna tell my father," the older boy asked, staring hard at me.

"Wade?" I asked, and he nodded.

"I'll leave that up to you. Don't come back here again."

"You're letting them off too easy," someone said from the crowd.

"I need to take care of Brady right now," I responded, "I can always talk to Wade if they cause more problems."

The boys jerked themselves out from under the hands of their captor and headed for the gate, arguing between themselves. I could well believe they didn't want to confront Wade with their behavior.

Turning to Tom, I placed my hand on his arm.

"I've been thinking, Tom, that your friends may be uncomfortable here without you," I said. "I'd hate to see the picnic cut short because of this. Perhaps it would be better if you stayed here and kept the picnic going. Bea and Jim will be here to help you."

"The grill's been hot for an hour," Bea interjected. "The corn is done. Let's get the meat going, and when you get back, you can tell us how Brady is."

"I'll go with you to the Vet's, Cathy," Mavis said. "I'm too old and stiff to play these games anyway."

"If that's what you want," Tom said slowly.

"There are padlocks in the kitchen drawer near the door. Would you padlock the kennel doors? I don't want to take any more chances."

"Right," Tom agreed, walking Mavis and me toward the gate as people began to move into little groups, talking quietly among themselves.

"This must have scared the kids. It's going to take a lot of energy to get the picnic going again," I commented.

"Ok, folks," Bea's voice boomed suddenly behind us, "who wants to help grill the meat? Anybody ready for food?"

Tom grinned down at me.

"I'll let her stir things up. She's got plenty of energy."

The ride to Dr. Barett's office distracted Brady from his wounded shoulder, and he hung out the window most of the way, letting the wind blow past his face and ruffle through his white collar.

"I don't know what to do about Sparky," I confided to Mavis. "I promised to take care of her, but I can't have her going into such rages that she bites."

"It's dangerous," Mavis agreed. "It could just as easily have been you that was bitten."

"I know," I said quietly. "She can be such a sweet dog. I didn't hesitate to take her. But I'm becoming afraid of her."

"Maybe you should just let Tom take care of her," Mavis suggested.

"She needs care every day. After today, Tom doesn't have any reason to be at the farm," I answered.

"Really? No reason? I would think you would be reason enough."

"Me?" I glanced away from the road for a quick look at her. She was studying me carefully, a little smile tugging at her lips.

"Tom is here doing a favor for Dr. Barett and John. And he knew Chase—all the guys are doing this for Chase."

"It may have started that way," Mavis said slowly, but with firmness. "But I think that if Tom hadn't liked you and wanted to get to know you, those fellas would have been finished with that fence in a couple of days."

I opened my mouth to tell her how wrong she was, but I couldn't speak.

Was she right?

"I don't know about that," I paused for a few seconds. "He's been very kind to me, but I didn't feel it was a personal interest."

"I've known Tom a long time," Mavis laughed. "I was his fourth grade teacher, you know. I've watched him grow into a man, become a soldier, get married, be injured, and go through hell. I think I know him well, and I think he's very interested in you."

"Well, I think he's a great guy."

"Tom was seriously injured. He has some pretty ugly scars. Does that bother you?"

"Why would that matter to me?"

"I've seen scars and disabilities bother some folks. They marry these handsome, sturdy, young partners who come back burned, missing limbs, brains scrambled. It's tough to handle."

"If Chase could have come back, I wouldn't have cared what condition he was in. I wanted him back the way he left, but I can't imagine not loving him because he wasn't perfect anymore."

"I think most partners feel that way. They're proud of their soldier, but faced with the daily care, the endless surgeries, so little support, or money, kids to care for, cramped quarters at hospital housing . . . . Some people can't make it. Some of the soldiers can't make it either, it really takes a toll on them."

"Thank God, Tom made it."

"Yes."

"I'm very confused about things right now," I shared. "I don't know what I really feel, and I'd hate to hurt him after what he's already been through."

"No, I don't want anyone hurting him again," Mavis agreed.

"You really like him."

"Harry and I, we both think the world of him."

I was silent then, and grateful that we were almost at Dr. Barett's clinic. I wondered if she had offered to come with me just to tell me that she thought Tom liked me. Was she trying to find out how I felt about Tom? Or was she just a romantic that liked to meddle, I wondered, as I pulled into the hospital parking lot.

"Don't complicate this," I told myself. "Just admit it. You like him and Mavis thinks he likes you. Say 'yes' to being alive again."

Dr. Barett didn't mince words with us.

"That bite tore the muscle in his shoulder," he said. "He needs the muscle stitched together or it will continue to tear, and he could be lame permanently."

Gently, he led Brady over to a cage in the surgical area and guided him into it, then turned back to me.

"Did Moose do this?"

I explained briefly about Sparky, the picnic and the neighbor boys letting the dogs out.

"Sparky hates Daisy and Daisy is terrified of her. I don't think it's good for them to be around each other at all, but I've promised to take care of them. I just don't know what to do except to keep them apart."

"Let me think about it, Cathy," he said, picking up Brady's chart. "Talk to me tomorrow. You can pick Brady up around three."

Mavis didn't bring Tom up to me again on the drive home, but she did keep up a steady chatter about herself and Harry and their children and grandchildren. I wished she would tell me something about Tom's ex-wife, or his marriage, but she didn't. I hesitated to ask, assuming she would tell him. Or she would tell Harry and Harry would tell him. Either way, questions could lead to a potentially embarrassing situation for one or both of us.

As we pulled into the driveway, I could hear the gentle twanging of a guitar and the soft singing of a group.

"I guess they got the party going again," I commented, and Mavis smiled.

"Bob brought his guitar. He never goes anywhere without it."

As we entered the back yard, Bob softened his guitar playing, and the singing died off as a sea of faces turned expectantly in our direction. Mavis gave my arm a squeeze and went off to join Harry and her grandkids. I saw Tom standing at the edge of the crowd with John Dunnom, who had arrived after Mavis and I had left. Smiling, I waved at them before speaking to the group.

"Brady needs a few stitches," I told the crowd. "The bite did tear the muscle, but he'll be home tomorrow. The vet doesn't expect any problems."

Bob gave his guitar a happy strumming and people clapped a little.

"We saw lots of deer," a child's voice yelled out.

"They were in your front yard, eating your roses," another child hollered.

I clapped my hands and laughed along with the others.

"How many did you see?" I asked.

"Five."

"Aren't they beautiful?" I questioned, looking at the excited children's faces.

"They were big," came the explosive answer.

"Big as horses," added another child.

"I'm so glad you saw them," I applauded.

I watched as the children milled around their parents and friends, still talking excitedly among themselves.

"We saved you ladies a little dinner," Harry's voice boomed.

He and Mavis had come up behind me. They walked with me over to the food table as Bob started playing another song, and the singing started again.

A grinning Bea, her arms linked to Jim on one side and Tom on the other, with John close behind, joined us a few seconds later.

"We waited to eat with you," she said, letting go of Tom's arm.

"Oh, good, I've never liked eating alone," I said, as Tom handed me a plate and took one for himself.

"How did it go?" he asked, "any problems?"

"Not really," I answered, looking in his eyes and letting myself feel the exciting energy that surrounded him. "Dr. Barett said we could pick Brady up tomorrow at three. He said he'd talk to me about Sparky then."

I knew that Mavis was right and so was Bea. Tom was interested in me. I could see it in his eyes. I could feel it in the way he took care of me. Why did I feel confused? I did like him. I wanted him in my life. Why couldn't I show it?

"I talked with Rob's sister," John's voice broke me out of my reverie. "All she knew was that her mother had gotten Daisy through a newspaper ad from a family in town, and that they did have other dogs there. But she didn't know what breed of dogs they were."

"Thanks for checking with her, John. But the handwriting is on the wall," I said. "I can't have Sparky around other dogs. She's too aggressive and unpredictable."

16

Husky Rescue

Tom rolled into my driveway at exactly two o'clock on Sunday. I had invited him to go with me to get Brady and talk with Dr. Barett. He had accepted immediately.

I had had a serious talk with myself the night before and with Chase this morning. Tom was right, I told Chase's picture. I have to go on living. I knew Chase wouldn't want it any other way. Even so, I felt disloyal. It felt strange to admit that I was interested in Tom and that he liked me. I felt anxious.

"You've been around him for weeks now," I told myself, watching him stride up the walk. "What are you nervous about?"

"Our relationship has changed. I don't know how to act on a date anymore."

"You're impossible," a part of me responded with irritation. "You like the man. Just act like you like him. You've done that already. Remember dinner? Try acting like Bea. Anyway, he doesn't think it's a date."

I tried. I gave his arm a little hug when he came in the door which seemed to surprise him. I could see it pleased him, and that he hadn't expected it.

During the trip to pick up Brady, I shared my concerns about how to tell Collette her dog had needed stitches because of Sparky.

"I'm thinking of not telling her at all until she gets back," I told Tom. "Brady's going to be fine. It seems to me that she has enough on her mind. Sparky's owner could be upset over it too."

"I'd support that," he said quietly. "What will you tell her about Sparky?"

"I've already told her that Sparky was too aggressive to be loose with the other dogs, and that I was going to keep him in a pen."

"Have you heard from the Private?"

"Not yet."

"Sometimes a soldier can't get to a message center for a few days, so I wouldn't let that worry me."

"You're right. I've got enough to fret about."

I saw the corners of his eyes crinkle in a stifled smile, as he glanced over at me. A gentleman, he didn't say the thought that I knew he'd had about me.

Dr. Barett greeted us with his usual warmth, patting my shoulder and shaking hands with Tom.

"Brady's fine and ready to leave," he advised us. "But I have some ideas I wanted to share with you."

"About what?" I asked.

"I called some friends, Arec and Peggy Meadows, last night," he said, leaning against the counter. "They have a farm north of here. I've known them for years, and they're good people. They've dedicated part of their farm as a Husky Rescue. I told them about Sparky, and they would be willing to keep her for your soldier friend."

"Oh, that would be wonderful," I gasped. "Isn't that great, Tom?"

"Sure is," he nodded. "That solves a big problem."

"They've worked with Huskies for years. They know how to keep them busy and happy. They run dog sleds in some of the Iditarod races in the winter."

"I wonder if Sparky has ever done that?"

"Well, she'll get a chance to learn. Huskies love to run," Dr. Barett shared, smiling, "especially in the snow."

"She'll love that," I said.

"Also, it sounds like you're ready to do some pet boarding."

"Well, we've got some great kennels set up," I answered. "I'm not all that sure of myself, but I'd like to try. Sparky kind of sapped my confidence."

"I could let you help out here for a few weeks in our kennel area. The techs could teach you a lot," he suggested.

"That sounds like a great idea," I enthused. "Thank you."

"Ok," he said. "Let me know when you want to start. Now, wait here. I'll get Brady for you."

Brady bounced into the room bringing an air of adventure and excitement with him. He whirled around the room, his eyes fixed on mine, his feet dancing.

"Getting stitches didn't seem to bother him any," Tom remarked, watching Brady's exuberant antics.

"He knows he's going home," Dr. Barett clarified with an amused smile.

"He's a happy dog, aren't you Brady," I said, drawing him to me so I could see his stitches.

"The inside stitches will dissolve," Dr. Barett commented. "The stitches you can see will probably fall out after a few days. If they're still there in ten days, bring him in, and we'll take them out."

As soon as Tom opened the door of the pickup, Brady squeezed past us and jumped in. He parked himself in the center of the front seat and looked around expectantly. Tom glanced at him, and looked down at me, preparing to climb in next to Brady.

"I think," Tom said slowly, "that he might be happier if he sat by the window, don't you?"

"Yes, he probably would." I responded quickly. "I wasn't thinking."

Tom took Brady's leash and called him. Brady stepped off the seat onto the floor of the cab, looking perplexed.

"I can get around him," I said, and started getting into the cab. Tom supported my arm as I slid onto the seat, squeezing my legs past the collie's side.

Tom closed the truck door, and Brady jumped back up onto the seat and settled next to me, his back straight against the cushions. Slowly he turned his head, and through the open window looked down his long nose directly into Tom's eyes.

I saw the expression in Tom's eyes change to one of incredulity.

"What happened?" I questioned.

"He just told me off," Tom said, laughing, and slapped the side of the truck. I heard him give a whoop as he went around the back of the truck.

"I'd rather sit next to you than that cocky dog," he muttered as he slid behind the wheel.

"I'm so flattered," I teased back.

★ ★ ★

I shut Moose, Brady and Daisy in the house the next morning. They showed their surprise at this turn of events by lining up at the windows to watch every step I took outside the house.

When I went to Sparky's pen, I could hear Daisy's roaring, frantic bark penetrate the morning air. Sparky glanced away from me toward the house and her ears flattened.

"I don't blame you, Sparky," I said quietly. "She makes an awful din. We're going to get you out of here so you don't have to listen to her anymore."

After putting Sparky in the car, I went back to open the doggy door. Daisy was still standing at the window, bellowing. I ignored her since she was so busy she didn't know I was there, but patted Moose and Brady as I left.

Tom had offered to go with me to the Meadows Ranch, fifty miles north of Traverse City. I quickly suggested picking him up as I came through the city. He had been to my home many times, but I had no idea where he lived.

It was a surprise to me when I saw the address was in an apartment complex of about fifteen interconnected buildings each one with four apartments. An apartment in the heart of the city didn't feel like the Tom I had gotten to know, even though it was only a couple of blocks from the beach. I guessed that Brenda had kept the house, and he had moved to the first available apartment he could find.

When I reached his address, I pulled out my cell phone to call him and let him know I was there, but his apartment door opened almost immediately.

"Mornin' Doll," he smiled, sliding into the passenger seat. "You look pretty today."

"Well, thank you," I said, "you look very handsome yourself. And," I added, "you really smell good. What is that?"

"Old Spice. You like that?" He answered. "My grandpa used to wear it."

"Your grandpa had style," I smiled.

"I was trying to find a way to be sure you noticed me more than the dogs," he laughed, glancing quickly at me as he pulled his seat belt across his chest and fastened it.

"Oh, no! I notice you, Tom. I really do," I grimaced in embarrassment. "I'm always more aware of you than the dogs, I swear."

"That's reassuring," he said, patting Sparky who had practically climbed over the back of the seat to greet him.

"I can't believe you thought that," I stammered, guiding my car back out to the street.

Tom turned his face away to look out the side window, and I couldn't see his expression.

"I guess I have been preoccupied with everything that's been going on," I added, hoping he would look at me again. I felt shut out by his movement away from me.

"A little," he turned back to me, smiling. "Don't worry about it."

Feeling reassured but slightly uneasy, I smiled back and turned onto the Coast Highway. The bay spread before us, partially hidden by a range of trees at the far end of the park. Dark blue water with rough waves capped in white foam in response to a strong wind and a sudden drop in temperature greeted us.

"The bay looks cold," I remarked idly.

"It doesn't feel like summer," he answered, his fingers drumming slowly but restlessly on his knee.

We drove in silence for a few miles, and I found myself feeling there was something different about him.

"Is there something bothering you, Tom," I asked finally. "You feel restless to me today."

"Oh?" he turned toward me and stretched his back a little, twisting back and forth a couple of times.

"Sorry. I'm fine. I've got a few aches today. I didn't sleep well last night, but it's nothing."

I nodded agreeably.

"So have you talked with the Meadows since I left you yesterday?" he asked, trying to open a conversation.

"Yes, last night for a few minutes," I answered. "Peggy Meadows gave me directions and told me they'd been rescuing Husky's for a few years. She sounded nice."

For several minutes we discussed the Husky Rescue and our hope that Sparky would be happy there, finally falling into a companionable silence.

Sparky rode to the Meadows Ranch sitting sideways on the back seat and gazing out the window. She seemed to enjoy being the only dog, occasionally nuzzling Tom's head for attention.

We turned off the highway onto County Line Road. As promised, two miles down this road we saw a large, hand-crafted wooden sign with "Meadows Ranch" etched into the wood and painted green. Below was a carving of a very alert Husky and the single word "Rescue." As we turned into the forest lane leading to the Ranch, Sparky became very alert.

"She must have gotten a whiff of animals out here," Tom remarked.

The dirt road followed a winding trail through the forest under sixty-foot-tall white pines towering overhead, their huge boughs shading the drive below. Occasionally, there was a lane branching off the road we were on, always with such a sharp curve we knew not to turn.

"Someone gave this road a lot of thought when they set it up," Tom remarked, after we had passed a couple of such curving lane turnoffs.

Ferns covered the forest floor, their bright green hues illuminating the rolling mounds of land they covered. Fallen tree trunks and branches scattered abundantly through the forest gave mute evidence to the wildness of the area.

We left the forest suddenly, driving into a clearing of waving green grass with only an occasional hardwood tree in view. We could barely see the forest growing larger in the very far distance.

"This clearing must be a half mile across," I observed.

"I think you're right," Tom replied. "It doesn't look like it's been cleared, but it's an unusually large area for a natural open space."

The lane turned abruptly from running along the edge of the forest to crossing the meadow. As we drove through the clearing, the warm sun overhead seemed to usher in an entirely different sensory experience. The air changed. The scents around us became sweet as if from flowers, although no flowers were in sight. In the distance, tiny buildings were coming into view.

Peggy Meadows was watering her lawn as we drove up. She smiled and waved us to a parking spot near the house, a two-story, updated farm home with a wide front porch the width of the building. Peggy herself appeared to be in her mid-forty's, athletically built, dressed in clean, pressed jeans cut off mid-calf, and a red and blue plaid blouse tucked in neatly at the waist. Her hair was brown and cropped close to her head. She had deep set brown eyes and a deep tan, already causing her skin to look a little weathered.

"You must be Cathy Maslin," she said, holding out her hand.

"I am," I said, taking her hand, "and this is Tom Ingalls."

Tom extended his hand and Peggy greeted him just as warmly.

"And this is Sparky, I'm guessing," she looked in the back seat at Sparky who was giving her a careful inspection with those reserved, calculating eyes.

As Tom opened the door to let Sparky out of the car, Peggy reached for her leash. Talking to Sparky in an upbeat voice, Peggy trotted her across the front yard and back again to the car. Sparky walked with her easily, keeping a curious eye on this new world around her.

"We do dog sledding here in the winter time," Peggy informed us. "The dogs love it, and it helps our income. Some people go for a dog sled ride, and they want their own sled and dogs. It helps to find homes for the rescued dogs."

"You did understand that Sparky only needs a home until his owner is back from active duty, didn't you?" I asked. "We wouldn't want you to be giving this dog to someone else."

"Yes, Dr. Barett shared that," Peggy said. "I talked with my husband about it. We're happy to help. We didn't know there was this kind of need."

"It was a surprise to me, too," I replied. "The soldiers are only too happy to pay their pet's expenses if someone will take good care of them."

"That's a help," Peggy stated. "Money to care for the rescues is always tight."

"How did you get involved in rescuing dogs?" I asked.

"We're being selfish," Peggy said, laughing. "We just love these dogs. Huskies are incredible animals. It was upsetting to see so many of them being put down by people who didn't know how to get the best from them. We wanted to help these dogs find good owners who understood their needs.

"Besides, we love riding dog sleds, and they love to run. Believe it or not, dog sleds can be very helpful in this part of the country in the winter."

Peggy had led us around the house and into the back yard as she talked. A couple of hundred feet ahead, we could see a huge red barn.

"The kennel is in the barn," she said. "They get very excited when they see a dog sled. That excitement can lead to a bit of aggression so we need lots of space."

"Well, Sparky can get aggressive, that's for sure," I commented wryly.

"Every dog has its likes and dislikes," Peggy asserted quietly, "just like people. Arec is in the barn. Let's go get him."

As we walked across the back yard, Arec, a gray-blond giant of a man, suddenly appeared in the barn doorway. Shaped like a triangle, Arec's broad shoulders tapered to a waist half the size of his shoulders. His denim shirt, open several inches down his chest, revealed a mass of curly gray hair. Black boots peeked out from beneath denim jeans covering mildly bowed legs.

"Welcome to the Meadows," he roared, reaching for Tom's hand. They shook hands like old friends, smiling and exchanging a few words I was too far away to hear clearly.

As his voice thundered through the air, I saw Sparky become instantly alert, aware of Arec's enormous energy. She glanced at me, her eyes curious and excited.

When Arec looked toward me, I waved my hand at him and smiled. He smiled and waved back, then glanced quickly at Sparky who was standing next to his wife.

Sparky was quiet but very alert, her tail moving slowly. When Arec knelt down and called her to him, she went to him quickly. Her eyes bright, she smelled his face inquisitively and then curled her body between his knees. She looked perfectly at home with him, and his huge hands stroked her gently.

"She's an old one," he commented suddenly.

"We understand she's at least ten years old," I responded. "She seems to be very healthy for her age."

"How does she run?" he asked.

"No one has run with her since she's been with me," I said. "I've had her for walks. She likes a good, fast walk."

"I'm taking her for a run right now. Let's see what she's got," and he took off with Sparky down the road. His huge frame moved with surprising grace and speed, but Sparky was ahead of him in two bounds. Together they raced down the road until all we could see was Arec's head bobbing above the tall grass.

Tom moved back to us chuckling, watching the race with amusement.

"Arec's going to have to move to keep up with Sparky," he laughed.

"Let's visit the kennels while they're running," Peggy suggested, gesturing toward the barn.

We had barely reached the kennels deep in the barn when Arec and Sparky raced up to us. Arec was puffing. Sparky was all smiles. Her tongue was hanging out, her eyes sparkling, her feet dancing with excitement.

"She's a runner," he exclaimed, wiping sweat from his brow with the side of his hand. "She'll love it here," he said to Tom and me.

"Let's put her in the kennel next to Karma," he said reflectively to Peggy. "She'll run well with him. I'm going to walk around with her a while."

Peggy nodded and motioned us to follow her through the kennels.

"He loves these dogs," was her only comment as he sauntered off with Sparky.

* * *

When we left the Rescue Center a couple of hours later, both Tom and I were pleased at how the dogs interacted with each other and with the Meadows. Sparky acted content in her new quarters and excited to be with other Huskies that she apparently recognized as her own kind.

As well as the individual kennels, about twelve dogs were paired together in small enclosures. Peggy explained that these were the dogs up for adoption.

"Some are dogs that we've bred and have been born here," she said, "although most are rescues. Our team dogs are kept on the other side of the kennel, over where Karma is. We don't want fights so we make sure they're paired well and have accepted their pack leader before they join a group."

"You're anticipating that Sparky will accept Karma as her pack leader?" I probed.

"Arec is really good at judging temperament and ability in a dog," Peggy answered. "If he thinks they'll get along, they probably will. Being kenneled right next to each other, they'll have plenty of time to get acquainted, and if there's a problem, it'll show up quickly."

"What do you think of Sparky?" I questioned. "Do you think she'll get along well?"

"You bet," Arec answered, coming up behind us, Sparky at his heel. His booming voice brought every dog to the front of its cage, excitedly watching him with eyes shining.

"They watch for every chance they can get to go for a run," he explained. "I take them out every day, but they'd run for days if they could.

"Sparky's going to do well here," he continued. "She's a neat little dog, good temperament, athletic, and very sociable. She won't have any troubles here. Being older, we'll put her with Karma's team. He's old and wise."

We left with assurances from them that they would keep in touch with Dave, and that we could visit Sparky if we wanted to see her. Peggy also shared that they would be open to fostering the Huskies of other service people who might need assistance.

"This was a good day's work," Tom commented as we left.

"It opened up some ideas to me," I shared. "I may contact other dog rescue groups if I hear of dogs I can't handle, or I don't have room for right then."

"They'd probably welcome the extra money from the owner to take care of them, too," Tom agreed.

As we neared his neighborhood, Tom suggested we stop at the beach for a few minutes and talk. I pulled into a parking area along the coast facing the water, and we sat quietly for a time, watching the sailboats gliding across the lake. The wind had died down, and the water, a deep, glittering blue reflecting the warm, afternoon sun, was moving softly toward the shore.

Tom sat silently, then rubbed his chin hard with the back of his hand and turned to me. His face was serious. His voice controlled. His eyes didn't quite meet mine as he started to speak.

"Cathy," he said, "I need to tell you something."

17

The Kennel

When I reached home that evening, I sat for a few moments in the driveway. It had taken all my strength to stay focused enough to drive home. I couldn't believe how the day had ended. I felt dazed, like I'd been hit hard in the head or was sick with a bad fever.

I could see the bears had been back, and the bird feeders lay in pieces on the ground. I didn't care. I'd take care of it another time.

The dogs were barking, staring at me through the fence. I didn't want to deal with them either. I felt so tired I didn't want to think. I didn't want to feel either.

Tom had taken me to dinner when we reached Traverse City. We were still thrilled about our visit to The Meadows. Sparky's excited reaction to the other Huskies dominated our conversation for some time. We really felt that the dogs were happy at the Meadows Kennel. I found myself pondering whether I would be able to encourage the same response in the dogs that might stay in a kennel I ran. Discussing Dr. Barett's offer to help me with my dog kennel led into a conversation about Tom's choices for his life now that he was a civilian again. Our conversation had dragged at times, but I had assumed that we were both distracted, even tired, by everything that had happened that day.

But after dinner, as we sat at the beach, he told me that he wouldn't be coming out to the farm again.

"I can't," he said, looking into my eyes, his expression serious. "You're not ready for a relationship, and I need to be more than just your friend."

He paused, as if waiting for me to say something, but I was too shocked to speak.

"I know what it's like to love someone and lose them," he continued. "I understand it's taking time for you to let go of Chase. I understand. But I've gotten too fond of you. I have to let go of you, at least for now."

He had leaned forward and kissed me on the mouth, a slow, gentle kiss that had set every nerve in my lips on fire. I could still feel his lips on mine an hour later.

"If you ever have room in your heart for another heart," he said, "call me."

He slid out of the car quickly and walked down the beach, his hands in the pockets of his jacket. I watched his back moving away from me, that familiar slight limp exaggerated by the soft sand

I hadn't been able to say a word, and I didn't know why. Part of my mind had screamed: "Don't go." "Kiss him back." "Grab his arm! He'll stay." But I had sat, frozen. When I could move; I had driven away. My mind was numb. My heart aching. I was totally confused by my behavior.

It was a dreamless night for me because it was also a sleepless night. I sat in my sunroom all night, staring outside. Three bears crossed my yard at different times during the night. They ambled around the yard, checked the birdfeeders smashed on the ground and moved on.

A bobcat took up residence on the roof of my car for a couple of hours. It disappeared as silently as it had arrived. Moments later, a raccoon left its hiding place and busily began to investigate the broken bird feeders. I heard an owl hooting somewhere in the woods. Deer tracked across my lawn in small groups several times, ate apples and roses and faded back into the forest.

Rabbits bounced through the yard, ate seeds and bounced out again. I knew the turkeys were roosting in the trees. The activity outside my window seemed more like a dull documentary than real life. I felt a total lack of interest in any of the animals or their behaviors.

Moose recognized my mood and sat stoically by the side of my chair. Daisy sat for a while at my feet, her chin resting on my foot, before finding a more comfortable place to spend the night. Brady lay under the window, alternately watching me with curious eyes and dozing.

My behavior didn't make a bit of sense to me. I had thought about Tom endlessly the last few days. I had already decided he was important to me, and that I wanted to spend time with him. I had made my peace with Chase. What had stopped me from reaching out to Tom? What was I waiting for?

So if Tom is who you want to be with, call him, I thought suddenly. It's not too late. Just pick up the phone, and call him. Inexplicably, I felt a strong resistance to calling him. Then the knowledge that this wasn't the right time for me to make such a decision filled my mind. That thought didn't solve my dilemma, but it did leave me with a sense of rightness. I closed my eyes as the sun was coming up and slept in my chair.

★　★　★

Moose jerked to his feet with a bellow, bumping my chair, just as the shrill peal of the doorbell tore through the house. I woke with a start, just in time to receive the full impact of Daisy leaping over my feet with a roaring bark that would have woken a body from their final sleep.

Disoriented, my nerves pounding, I glanced out the window and saw Wade pacing on my front porch.

"Oh, boy," I thought, staggering to my feet. As I moved into the living room, I saw Brady, calmly curious and still chewing on a breakfast snack, slowly exiting the kitchen to see what the fuss was about.

I took a deep breath as I reached the front door and then opened it. The dogs crowded around my knees, still barking.

I gave Wade a nod and turned my attention to the dogs.

"Stop," I commanded. "Back." I motioned them away from the door and, grumbling, they did as they were told.

"I'm always amazed," I said to Wade through the screen, "when they do what I tell them."

He gave the briefest of smiles, glanced quickly at me and back to the dogs.

"What brings you out so early today, Wade?" I asked, still attempting a friendly demeanor.

He cleared his throat and looked dead into my eyes. His body hunched forward, his hands in the back pockets of his jeans. His body position was both threatening and cowed at the same time.

I wished I'd slept better the night before. My eyes felt pinched and tired, my mind was a bowl of fog, and I had to talk with Wade. It was enough to give a normal person the shudders.

"Last night, Lee told me that you told him he wasn't welcome down here," he said, his face grim. His eyes looked piercingly at me. "What's he done?"

"Oh," I said, struggling for the right words.

"If he did something bad over here, I'll thrash him," Wade spit out. "I don't want no trouble with my neighbors."

His words cleared the fog from my mind in a second as the hardness of the boys' faces flashed through my memory.

"I don't want you 'thrashing' him, Wade," I asserted. "They weren't being mean."

"So why did you throw them out?"

My mind raced through the ramifications of telling it like it happened, or soft peddling the incident. Too many people involved, I decided. I'd better stick to the truth and hope I could talk him out of hitting the kids.

"They came down during our picnic and, thinking they were lonesome, let the dogs out of their kennels. A visiting dog bit Brady."

"I'll thrash 'im. He knows better than to let dogs loose."

"No, Wade," I felt annoyed at his medieval approach to parenting. "I sent them home and told them not to come back without an invitation. They could have had a good time, and they were sent home. That's enough."

"I don't think so," he said empathetically. "They got to learn to be men."

"Beating on them isn't going to turn them into men."

"Oh, you don't think so? Than what will?"

A belligerent note had crept into his voice, and I felt Moose bristling under my hand.

"Teaching them to be responsible," I paused, thinking for a moment. "Look, Wade, suppose when the kennels need cleaning, I'll give you a call, and you can send them down to clean the kennels a couple of times."

"They'll understand better if I take a switch to them."

"That'll work off your anger at them, but it doesn't teach them anything about how to make amends when they make a mistake. Can't you see that?"

Wade was silent, looking off into the distance.

"I know their behavior is disappointing, Wade. But they are just kids. They still have a lot to learn."

"Ok," he said finally, as he turned to leave. "We'll do it your way this time. But they're my kin, and I want them behaving. I don't want no problems with neighbors."

"I understand completely," I said, wondering what he thought his previous encounters with me had been.

I said a quick prayer that he wouldn't beat on the boys and reached down to pat the excited, squirming bodies surrounding my knees.

★   ★   ★

Over the next few days, I cleaned closets, kennels, the yard, and went for a daily run in the woods around the house. I polished everything in the house that I could reach and slowly confirmed to myself that I was going to need more in my life than I had.

It was too late to plant a garden and expect to get a harvest, but I spent a few hours planting an iris bed outside the kennels. I built a small rock garden near the bird feeders, tucking pots of already blooming impatiens, lavender, and carnations into the crevices.

I finally called Dr. Barett, reminding him of his offer to let me volunteer at his office for a few weeks. In his usual caring way, he instantly welcomed me aboard his staff, inviting me to start the next day.

When I arrived the next morning, his assistant, Jackie, welcomed me just as warmly.

"You already know how this office works," she laughed, her brown eyes snapping, "so we're expecting a really fast learning curve from you."

"Stop it," I widened my eyes and made a face. "You're scaring me."

Jackie couldn't have been more helpful over the next few days. She kept me right with her for the first couple of days, explaining every procedure and action that she performed.

Since she had worked for Dr. Barett for seventeen years, and the two often communicated without words, the detailed descriptions were really important to me. A couple of times, Dr.

Barett had listened to her clarification of an office procedure with rapt attention.

"I often wondered," he said, grinning slyly, "why we did things that way."

"He knows. He's a big tease," Jackie said, laughing.

Over the next few days I cleaned and disinfected cages and kennels until my hands and back ached. Unbelievably, I reached a place where I no longer smelled the disinfectant.

I learned how to move annoyed cats from one cage to another without being bitten or scratched. I also learned that I felt real fear around some dogs.

"It's something about their energy or their eyes," I tried to explain to Dr. Barett. "They look aggressive to me. I feel scared of them."

"Any dog can be dangerous if it's frightened or sick," asserted Dr. Barett. "You have to show the dog, through your voice and behavior, that you have the authority. The dog is not on his own turf. He knows he's in your space. So if you show the dog you're in charge, he won't have to challenge you for dominance."

I nodded my head, attempting to muster up my confidence, but silently I made a resolution not to board any dog that scared me.

After a few weeks, Dr. Barett told me I had graduated his clinic.

"You know what to do to keep animals safe, clean and cared for," he told me. "You know how much to feed different animals and when they need medical attention."

"I'm pretty sure I'm taking better care of the dogs than I have been," I replied. "But I'm learning something new every day I'm here."

"If you're not sure about something, be sure to call. We'll always have time for you," he said gently. "You're opening a kennel, not a hospital. You know what you don't know, and sometimes that's the most important information you can have."

"If you ever need to give Jackie a day off, I'd love to help," I told him.

"You're on," he said, giving me a hug.

Jackie also gave me a hug, a ton of compliments about how competent I was, and good wishes for my kennel.

The excitement of someday soon having a successful kennel kept my spirits soaring in spite of the sadness I felt leaving the clinic. I was heartened by the idea of filling in for Jackie on occasion. I had loved being a part of the office. It made me lonesome for the camaraderie I had felt as a teacher in school.

Two days later, Dr. Barett referred a couple who needed to board their two Pugs. His clinic's boarding facilities were completely booked. The couple, Monte and Sherry Whitman, had received an unexpected call that Monte's mother was seriously ill in another city several states away. They had to leave immediately, and they had to find a safe haven for their pets while they were away.

The Whitmans arrived at the farm with their Pugs the next day. The dogs, Chloe and Mike, were about the size of Moose's head, weighing only about fifteen pounds apiece. Their barrel-shaped, wide-chested, fawn-colored bodies were in sharp contrast to their strong black muzzles and large, brown, luminous eyes. The deeply set wrinkles around their eyes gave them a look of concerned wisdom.

When we had talked on the phone the day before, I had suggested Sherry bring the Pugs' favorite toys and a blanket to keep them company. The Whitmans arrived loaded with their dogs' belongings. They had brought a blanket from their own bed as well as a large, round, pet bed with a sunken area to sleep in. Squeekies, balls, and cloth chew toys, a bag of their food, and their own dining bowls were in their box of goodies.

"We've never left them with anyone before," Sherry confided to me, "but this is one time we just can't take them with us. We're pretty worried about leaving them with someone they don't know."

"They'll be fine," I assured her, "but if I see the slightest problem, I'll call Dr. Barett."

"They've never been outside for any length of time," she added.

"They can be inside or outside whenever they want," I explained. "They're so small, if I see they're uncomfortable, I'll bring them into the house. But most dogs really like the outdoors."

Sherry nodded and smiled, but continued to chew on her lower lip. I knew my answer had only partially assuaged her concerns.

Monte was concerned about Moose.

"He's a very big dog," he said finally. "He won't have access to our dogs, will he?"

"My dogs will be able to visit from outside the kennel," I said, "but they won't be able to reach Mike and Chloe physically."

Monte stared at the chain link fence, unconvinced.

"Moose is very protective," I assured him. "He wouldn't hurt another dog. I'm absolutely sure of that."

They left with assurances that I would be happy to hear from them every day they wanted to call. I also promised that I would play a tape of their voices for the Pugs daily.

The Pugs turned out to be a delight to have at the ranch. Chloe and Mike adapted nicely to kennel life. They showed their enjoyment of visits from the big dogs by pawing through the fence to touch the other dogs. They barked and whined when the other dogs were outside, but hadn't visited them. Both Chloe and Mike were voracious eaters, devouring everything placed in front of them. They slept cuddled together in their pet bed, entangled in the Whitmans' blanket.

Throughout the evening, I did worry about them outside at night with so many unknowns in the forest. About ten o'clock, already through my evening preparations for bed, I stood at my bedroom door, feeling restless and uncomfortable. They were so small. What if a bobcat went over the fence?

I finally decided to compromise. With Moose, Brady and Daisy trotting behind me, I went out into the cool night air and brought them inside. I would keep them inside at night, I decided, and take them back outside in the morning. I fixed them a place to sleep in the downstairs spare bedroom. They took the change in stride and I slept better with them in the house.

Moose, Brady and Daisy, extremely curious about the Pugs, took turns sleeping in my bedroom and outside the Pugs' bedroom door.

I learned a great deal from the Pugs' visit. I needed a counter area with water faucets in the barn if I was going to feed and water animals there. Water was available through a hose, but inconvenient to use.

Woody, the neighborhood handyman, who had helped with various projects around the house in the past, agreed to build the counter I wanted.

My second awareness was that if I wanted to board small dogs, I would need an area prepared in a safe place. I didn't want to worry about them being eaten by some wild critter when I wasn't looking.

I also recognized that a bear could easily break into the barn, and a wild cat could clear the fences if properly motivated. I wondered if any dog, short of a Rottweiler, was actually safe in the kennels. I needed to make some changes if I was going to continue with the kennel project.

"I think," Woody told me when I shared my thoughts with him, "that I'd cover the three kennels with fencing so the dogs couldn't climb out and nothing could climb in. Then I'd reinforce the walls in the barn with cross beams and put in better fitting doors with locks. That should do it."

"Let's go ahead with covering the kennels, Woody," I said, thinking of my overworked bank account. "I want to think more about securing the barn."

"I'll get it done tomorrow," Woody answered.

I liked Woody. He was on the short side, wiry, and probably in his mid-fifties. His sun-wrinkled face and grayish-black hair spoke to endless hours in the out-of-doors. He was a master craftsman, happily married, with two teen children still at home. He was a happy man, quick with banter and double entendres that I rarely "got" at the time he said them, which delighted him.

His ideas for the barn seemed sound to me, but I questioned if the barn would really be warm enough for small dogs. I wondered, too, if there was a less expensive way to fortify the barn, at least until I had money coming in.

The garage was just big enough for the car and washing machine. The pole barn would cost a fortune to insulate and turn into a small animal kennel. I knew, too, that I wouldn't want to be going out there every day in the winter. It was too far from the house. Some winter days could be really unpleasant to walk any distance at all.

That left the house.

There were three bedrooms and a bath upstairs that were virtually unused. A master bedroom and bath, a spare room, and a hallway bathroom, were downstairs. A single story wing of the home held a dining room between the kitchen and living room, and a sunroom off the living room. There was also a large room off the kitchen with several windows, apparently used as a work room by the previous farm owners.

Chase and I had planned to make this large area into a family room. It had an outside door and extended across the entire width of the house. It was big enough to hold several work tables, two of which were still there. They were large, rugged, wooden tables with heavy legs, the tops stained by countless liquids.

When Chase had first moved into the farmhouse, we had cleaned every room, washing walls and scrubbing floors. Then, room by room, we had worked on painting, furnishing, and decorating.

We had cleaned this back room and then locked the door, leaving it for last, for when Chase came home. Then we would make our family room dream come true. A couple of times a year, I would go out and dust the ceiling of cobwebs that might be forming. I would wash the windows and floor, and dust the tables, but that was all the attention it had gotten. Now it was time to turn the room into a work place again.

It turned out to be an enormous task for one person. By dinner the next day, I had the windows taped, the walls and woodwork primed, and I was exhausted.

Even with the radio going, it was lonesome work. Moose, Brady and Daisy took turns coming into the room to watch me. Although the windows were open, they didn't like the smell of the paint. The odor soon drove them back outdoors.

The next day, I pushed myself to paint the walls and woodwork. I didn't have enough of one color of paint to do all the walls, so I painted each wall a different color. The big wall became the blue of my kitchen. The opposite wall had the windows, and I painted this wall off-white. One of the end walls, I coated a buttercup yellow, and put sage green on the other. It was clean and oddly cheerful.

"Pick out what you want for linoleum," Woody said, handing me a piece of paper with the floor measurements. "Just be sure they have enough on hand to deliver by Friday morning. They need to put it in the room 'cause it's heavy stuff. I'll go in Wednesday and pick up the luan boards to have the floor ready."

I ate dinner, fed the dogs, brought the Pugs in, soaked in the tub for a half hour, and went to bed, muscles still aching. I would have to clean the back yard and kennel the next day before going to Traverse City. Maybe Bea would be free for lunch. I needed a break!

18

Room For Another Heart

The Whitmans called the next morning while I was getting breakfast. They were concerned about their dogs and delighted to know Mike and Chloe were staying in the house at night.

I assured them that there had been no eating problems or digestive disturbances. The Pugs had had no physical contact with my dogs, I told them, adding that they were just delightful visitors to my home. I found myself sharing their enthusiasm for the little dogs. The Pugs' sturdy, inquisitive, and gregarious dispositions had become a source of enjoyment for me.

★   ★   ★

Bea was at The Northwoods Inn when I arrived. One of our favorite restaurants, windows as wide as the booths, ran the entire length of the dining room. Every window overlooked the Bay, always alive with sailboats, swans, ducks, and beach denizens.

Fashioned after a log cabin, even the inside walls were rough-hewn logs. The floor was paved with uneven bricks. Deer, moose, and bear heads adorned the high walls along with a fox, a beaver, snow shoes, skis, and primitive farming tools. A full grown bear was mounted in a corner of the bar.

At either end of the large dining room was an immense rock fireplace, one of which was complete with a huge black caldron.

In addition to the rustic ambiance, the food was exceptional, and the desserts a delicious meal in themselves. We had often agreed that this was not a restaurant that catered to dieters.

Bea had chosen a booth at the windows near the far fireplace. True to her nature, I could see that her energy was bubbling over. Her fingers were tapping. Her legs were crossed with the top leg waving as she talked and laughed with a waiter. He was just as animated, waving one arm, a dish in his other hand. He was rocking on one leg while talking jovially, as he and Bea shared about whatever grand topic had come to life between them.

We were going to have excellent service, I told myself. It was a good thing we were meeting for a late lunch, and most diners had already left. From the looks of things, this young man had other things on his mind than work.

I interrupted their chatter as I arrived at the table and sat down. The waiter looked at me, seeming surprised, and turned to Bea.

"Oh, it's a 'she'," he declared. "I would have thought it would be a 'he' you were waiting for."

They both laughed as if that was the funniest thing that could be said in the English language. I just felt annoyed.

"She has a 'he' at home," I offered dryly, ending their party and squashing any hope of excellent service for me.

"You can be so dull sometimes," Bea chided me, shaking her head. "Laugh a little. It won't hurt you."

"Have a nice lunch," the waiter said, handing us menus. With raised eyebrows, he rolled his eyes in Bea's direction.

"I saw that," I said to Bea when he had left our table.

"I know," she giggled. "I'm such a fun person, and you're so grumpy he feels sorry for me."

"I didn't think I was grumpy," I defended myself. "I just made a statement of fact and you called me dull."

"Facts aren't funny," Bea asserted, "but I'll tell you something that is. Jim ran into Tom yesterday at the market. They've really hit it off."

"How is that funny?" I asked, staring at the suddenly blurred menu.

"Jim suggested that you and Tom join us for dinner this weekend. Tom declined. So Jim did a little probing. He learned that you and Tom have broken up."

"Broken up? We've never gone together," I declared, astonished.

"Why haven't you? Tom's a nice man," Bea pushed. "What's the matter with you?"

"Bea," I laid the menu down and looked her straight in the eyes. "Did Tom say we'd broken up, or is that your spin on what he said?"

"Ok, it's my spin," Bea admitted. "He said the work was done out there, and he's been busy in town. He said that if you needed him for anything, you'd call, and you haven't called."

"That's the truth."

"But why? I know you like him. I know he likes you. What's it going to take to get you two together?"

"It's hard to explain, Bea. I'm lonesome. I miss Tom. But I don't know if I miss Tom for Tom, or if I just miss having a man around. I just don't know."

"What does it matter?" Bea asked seriously.

"It matters. He's been hurt a lot in life. I don't want to hurt him too."

Bea was silent for a minute, leaning forward over the table, listening closely to me.

"He's a great guy, but I became dependent on him so fast. I need to know I can get along without his support. That I want him for him, and not for what he can do for me, not just because I need something."

Bea leaned against the seat back; her eyes watched me, unwavering. I knew she had heard me clearly.

"Cathy, I think you're in love with him," she said quietly.

"He's important to me," I admitted. "I don't know that I love him. I really like him. I like the way he thinks. I like his sense of humor. I do miss him. But . . . it's just not the right time, Bea."

"When is it going to be the right time?"

"I don't know. But right now feels wrong."

"Ok, I won't press you anymore," she said, picking up the menu again.

"Let's eat. Now tell me what you did with the Husky."

★ ★ ★

Woody arrived late the next morning with his pickup truck loaded with luan. It looked like plywood to me.

"Look what I found yesterday," I said. "I went to the Electronic Village in Traverse. It's a motion detector. If anything crosses the beam, it sets off an alarm. We can set it up around the sides of the barn. If an animal tries to get in, it should be scared off."

"I've seen these before," Woody mused, poking around at the box of gadgets I held out to him. "Don't know why I didn't think of it. I'll set it up after I paint the ceiling. I think it should be about two feet off the ground so it doesn't go off if a skunk or rabbit passes by."

I was about to answer when the phone rang.

"I thought I'd check and see how Daisy is doing," Rob said. "Sorry I haven't been in touch earlier."

"It's ok, Rob. John explained what happened, and I've gotten your checks," I assured him. "Daisy is a delight. She's such a happy dog. I don't think her tail ever stops wagging."

Rob laughed, an easy, male chuckle that made me smile.

"She is a happy dog," he agreed. "Mom always said that too."

"How is your mom?"

"Doing better," a sober note had crept into his voice. "The doctors are optimistic."

"I am so glad, Rob. This has to be hard on her and all of you."

"A stroke can do some real damage. But we're hopeful. She's a toughie!"

"Well, I hope she's fully healed soon. I wanted to ask you something about Daisy. A Husky came to me from a soldier in Cadillac. Daisy was very fearful around her. I had the feeling they knew each other from somewhere else. Do you know where your Mom got Daisy?"

"Not really," Rob answered. "I was away. Mom said that when she first saw Daisy, she looked pretty beaten up. She was small, very thin and nervous. Mom thought that she probably had to fight for food and felt really sorry for her. She took her even though she was a bit scared of Shepherds."

"I can see the nervousness when she gets barking."

"Yeah. How is she getting on with the Husky now?"

"Sparky is staying at a Husky Rescue about fifty miles north of Traverse. I didn't want to be responsible for the two of them here together. They were only around each other a couple of days, but both dogs were really stressed."

"That's probably wise."

"Daisy is a sweet dog. I want her to be happy here."

"I'm glad you like her. I'm going to be gone for quite a while, so if this is working out, she'll be with you for a few more months at least."

"Don't worry about her, Rob. She has a home here as long as she needs it. Give me an address where I can reach you. I'll send you pictures and keep you updated on what's going on with her."

After our call ended, I went back to see how Woody was doing. He was balanced on one foot at the top of a ladder, leaning out precariously to reach the area he was painting. I was afraid to speak for fear he would lose his balance.

"Woody, what are you doing?" I asked when he had both feet on the ladder again.

"Painting," he said, looking at me quizzically, and waving the paint brush.

"But you could fall stretched out like that," I protested.

"Na, not me," Woody grinned. "I've built skyscrapers when I was younger. I've got great balance. Me, I'm not afraid of heights or falling."

"I'm afraid for you."

"Then don't watch," Woody laughed.

"I want that in writing for my insurance company," I tossed over my shoulder as I left the room.

Even though I didn't stay in the room, I decided to remain in the house in case he did fall and needed help. I liked Woody. I liked his work, but I didn't like the risks he was taking. I had stood on the tables and walked back and forth to paint the high areas of the walls. Woody could have used the tables more safely than the rickety ladder he was using. I wondered how Tom would have painted the ceiling.

I settled down the hall at my computer to pay bills and work on my budget. I was close enough to hear a crash if ~~Harry~~ *Woody* fell, and I fully expected it could happen.

I was glad Rob had called. I had liked Rob on sight, and I was surprised when he had left Daisy so abruptly and failed to check on her at all. But Daisy wasn't his dog, I reminded myself. He was in a dangerous job with an erratic time schedule and a seriously ill mother.

When Woody left for the day, the ceiling was painted without incident, and Luan covered over half the room. The linoleum would be delivered in the morning. The indoor kennel was taking shape, and the barn was wired with motion detectors.

★ ★ ★

The Whitmans called again the next morning. Their trip was on schedule. Everything was going well for them. Against all odds, Monte's mother was improving.

"I put your blanket in the bedroom for Chloe and Mikey to sleep on, but this morning I found them curled up asleep on the bed," I told them. "I think they're quite comfortable and making themselves at home."

They hung up the phone, sounding happy and relieved.

★ ★ ★

Early the next week, I finally heard from Pvt. Dave Seymour. His email was terse.

Dear Mrs. Maslin:

Couldn't write before now. Been out. How is Sparky? Collette told me she was getting into some kind of trouble. Would like the particulars. Collette gave me an address where to send money and will get that arranged pronto.

Pvt. David Seymour

I emailed him back immediately.

Dear Pvt. Seymour

Sparky and another dog hated each other on sight, and almost fought. Then Sparky bit still another dog so fiercely it needed stitches. The bill was $114.00 for the vet. It was too dangerous and stressful to have her staying here. Sparky is now with Arec and Peggy Meadows at the Meadows Husky Rescue. They raise Huskies and are into dog sledding. Sparky is happy there. You can reach Arec and Peggy at <u>meadowsdogsled@united.com</u>. They are expecting your call. They assured me they will care for Sparky until you return for her. Please send me $175 to cover the vet bill, costs to get her out of the Cadillac Shelter, and for gas to take her to the Husky rescue. That will cover the expenses we've had for her.

Mrs. Maslin

I didn't hear from the Private again, but two days later found a deposit in my bank account for $175.00.

The Whitmans picked up the pugs that same day. Chloe and Mike were ecstatic to see their lost owners. Their little, square bodies just danced and bent in ways I wouldn't have imagined possible as they greeted the Whitmans.

"They don't look any the worse for wear," remarked Sherry as she picked Mikey up to give him a hug. "They seem to have handled being away from us just fine."

"Yes, they did well," I smiled at her candor. "I know they missed you, but I think they really enjoyed the new experiences they had here."

★ ★ ★

Dr. Barett called the next day and congratulated me on my success with my first boarders.

"They were really pleased with the care you gave their dogs," he related. "They had no complaints about anything. You've done a good job, Cathy."

★ ★ ★

Two weeks later, I collapsed into my favorite chair in the sunroom with a cup of coffee for a well-earned break from the day's activities. Dr. Barett and the Whitmans had sung praises for my kennel to the right people.

I had three magnificent, larger dogs boarding with me. A family of two Golden Retrievers shared one kennel. A Boxer claimed the middle kennel. In the house kennel, a French Bulldog and a Dachshund were working on my heartstrings.

Every one of these dogs had a different personality, needing attention and affection. Each one was a paying boarder. I loved caring for the dogs. I enjoyed their responsiveness to me and observing their curiosity as they experienced new situations and animals they hadn't met before.

Moose, Brady, and Daisy traveled from dog to dog doing their share to keep everyone entertained and in good spirits.

I had carved out a busy life for myself. Thankfully, I was again on the way to earning a living, which made me feel more secure. I felt proud of myself for these accomplishments, but I missed the companionship I had felt at Dr. Barett's Veterinary Hospital.

Relaxing in the sun-drenched room, I watched the birds flitting about the bird feeders. As I relaxed, I began to think about Tom and Chase and what could have been with each of them. Thinking of the life Bea and Jim had together only reminded me of what I was missing. Even though I was happy with what I was building, I wanted so much more from life.

Then I saw the wasp. Circling the rose bushes, buzzing from one blossom to the next, never satisfied enough to sit and rest. What was his search about now?

I watched as the wasp touched first one rose and then another. Each time exploring between the pedals, dipping down into the softness of the bud, to rise again, circle again, and flit to another blossom.

This time I didn't want to watch the wasp. I closed my eyes, feeling a helpless wave of emotion passing through my chest. I couldn't settle down either, I lamented to myself.

My life was easing past me, a day at a time, while I expended my energies on whatever was in front of me to do. Why? What was I looking for?

Why wasn't I able to make the choices I wanted to make from the depths of myself?

Was I trying to prove an independence that was, perhaps, only a way to explain the passage of time? Was I waiting for someone who couldn't come back to me again? There was only one Chase. He was gone forever, and I knew it in my mind and in my heart.

I looked again at the wasp, certainly the most unlikely source of inspiration. Was this creature my teacher? It was now flitting about the blossoms of a different rose bush.

Everyone has their own special pains and sorrows they have to live through and go on, I reminded myself. What made me feel so different? Why was I so unwilling to let go of the past? Why was I so critical of the present?

What did I need to *know* about myself to make peace with myself, to make peace with life, and to move on?

How were my *needs* different from my *wants*?

I *needed* to know, I told myself slowly, that I was strong enough, smart enough, to survive the problems of my life, whatever they were, and alone if necessary.

I *wanted* to love a special man and to be loved by him.

I *knew* I could not protect myself from hard times and still live the life that I wanted to live.

It was time, and I knew it was time, to make the call. Tom was the only man in two years who had become important to me, whose character and humor had resonated in my heart. I needed, and wanted, to have him in my life.

I waited, feeling breathless, as his phone rang.

Hearing Tom's voice for the first time in weeks brought an excitement and a sense of rightness to my soul.

"Tom?" I said, hearing the tension in his voice as he answered.

"Cathy?"

"Yes. Um . . . It's me. How have you been?" I asked, feeling hesitant.

"Ok," he answered, then added quickly. "It's been quiet up here. Just doing the usual. Nothing new here."

I was grateful for his statement. "Nothing new. Just the usual." I translated that to mean, "No, I don't have a girlfriend."

"Tom, I've missed you. I . . . I have room for another heart now."

He was quiet for a heartbeat.

"You're sure?"

"I want it to be you."

"I'm leaving now. I'll be there within the hour."

"I'll be here."

I hung up the phone, my hand trembling, my face wet with sudden tears.

Moose had been nearby, his soft brown eyes watching me. He seemed to be aware of the strong emotions I had been feeling the last few days. He came close, and I wrapped my arms around his neck and gave him a hug.

"He's on his way, Moose. He's on his way."